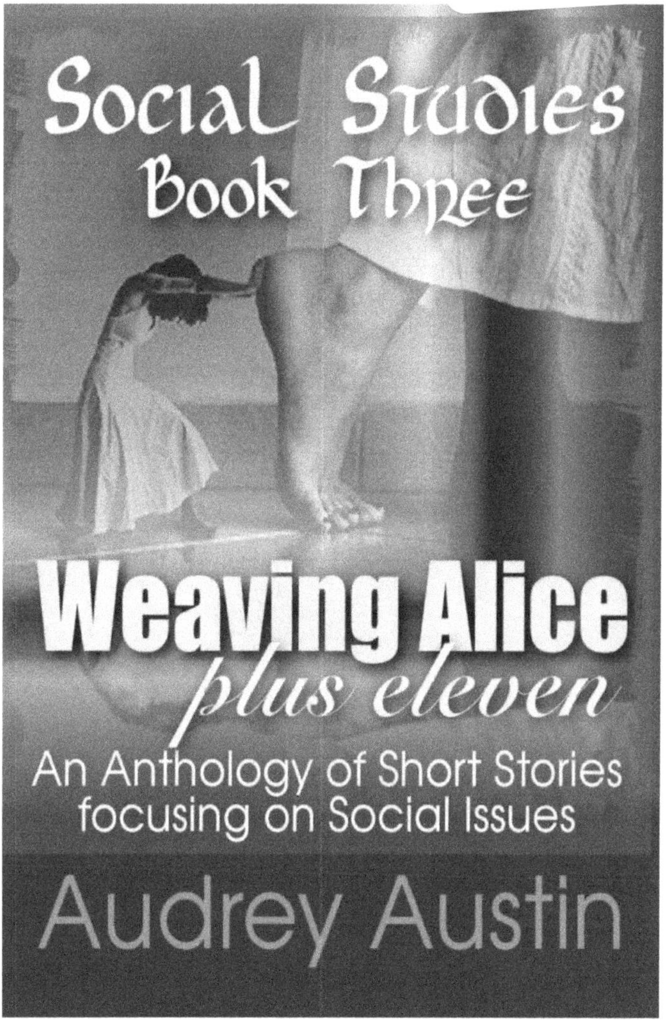

Social Studies
Book Three

Weaving Alice
plus eleven

An Anthology of Short Stories
focusing on Social Issues

Audrey Austin

SOCIAL STUDIES

Book Three – Weaving Alice Plus Eleven

Also for your reading pleasure:

Book One – Dying To Be Popular Plus Eleven

Book Two – Shattered and Broken Plus Eleven

A Trilogy of Anthologies

Short Stories

Which keep the focus on

Social Issues

Written and compiled by

Audrey Austin

2

SOCIAL STUDIES

This is Book Three of a trilogy of anthologies containing short stories focused on Social Issues.

Cover design by Susan Ruby K.; Yuneekpix.com

ISBN 978-0-9937163-0-0

Other Books by Audrey Austin

Sara, a Canadian Saga

The Silent Star Plus a Dozen

Reawakening

Keeping It Simple

Ellen and The Hummingtree

Moose Road – a Canadian Tragedy

Beyond The Blue

Recompense

When God Gives Us Spring

Social Studies, Books 1 and 2

TABLE OF CONTENTS

WHEN BUBBLES RISE

"I was warned. What more can I say? I was warned and now I pay the highest price!"

"My dear woman, I share your pain. Tell me your story. Give your anguish to God and find space within your soul for peace to find a home once more."

"I cannot speak of home. Please, Father, I beg of you; do not force me to talk of the past. I cannot. I will not."

"My child, you must trust me. I am here to listen. This is your opportunity to lift the heavy burden from your heart. You are a young woman. Free yourself of this weight and one day you will be able to leave this hospital to begin a new life."

"I cannot speak of these things."

"If you cannot tell me your story, then I accept that you cannot. I will leave you now but before I go, my child, accept this from me. This book is filled with many blank pages. This pen which I hand to you now is filled with my prayer; one that will be answered when you find the courage to write down all that has happened. God bless you, my child. Peace be with you."

And he did leave as he said he would. Why does he talk about peace when, for me, there is nothing but the noise of godforsaken barrenness? I am an empty shell and I sit here in this lonely laboratory like a rat trying to escape dissection by the constant, incessant questioning of poor priests and piercing psychiatrists. Why can't they just leave me alone?

I need to be alone. I am afraid to be alone.

And then the heart-wrenching awareness of my aloneness spills like a big wave over my hurting heart. God has no use for one such as me. God has stolen my Gabriela and when I ask Him why, there is no answer. It is my entire fault and God blames me. I was warned but I refused to listen.

I stare down at the pen that Father Morales gave to me. It looks like a very ordinary ballpoint pen except for the words, *Homes in Arakoon.* I have heard the nurses whispering and I know all about Father Morales' recent return from a vacation in Australia. Did he ever dream that this token of remembrance would wind up in the helpless hands of a wretch like me in Talcahuano Hospital's psychiatric ward?

I am holding the pen in my hand. I lift the pen up to my ear and listen. The prayer it carries is silent. If I were to step into this silence and allow it to carry me back to my Gabriela who would stop me? Who would apply the brakes and prevent me from being where I long to be?

I keep holding the pen and soon I begin to feel the warmth of the prayer. Is it possible? Of course it is not possible, I tell myself. I am a lunatic; a crazy woman. Warm prayers are not for spirits like me who are cold at the core. My punishment is to continue an empty existence incapable of feeling; unworthy of death.

Yet I feel the warmth of the prayer in the pen which I hold in my childless, right hand.

Find the courage to write it down. Yes, those were Father Morales' words. With my left hand I reach down and lift the book. I allow it to enter into my miserable mind. I see that it is a very ordinary journal with an extraordinary violet cover. I stare at this cover until Gabriela's violet eyes stare back at me. I am buried beneath the gossip of seven years ago when my Gabriela was a babe in my loving arms.

"The child of an Aymara mother with violet eyes?" the women of Talcahuano question. "This is no miracle! This is a curse!"

"Where is the child's father?" the men ask their wives.

"We will know him by his eyes." the women reply.

"This child is not one of us!" the men decree. "This child is an outcast!"

I stare at the violet cover of Father Morales' book and my head is crowded with the unwanted jeers aimed at an unwanted baby; unwanted by her violet-eyed, Canadian father; unwanted by her Aymara community.

Unwanted by me?

No, I cannot consider these things. My Gabriela was my life. I loved my little girl. I want my child!

Something in the dark recesses of my mind screams. "You didn't want the child. You were warned."

In my mind's eye I see my mother, Maria Soto. She is shaking her finger in front of my face and her shame falls from her finger deep into my soul. "You have disgraced the family. Your belly will grow big and where is the father? I warned you to stay with your own kind. How can I hold up my head?"

My head pounds with the memory. *Write it down*, he had said.

And I sit on the edge of my bed with a prayerful pen in one hand and a book in the other. I open the book and I see the pages are blank except for the lines which invite words to rest upon them. What do I know of writing? What do I know of syntax or spelling or speaking the truth?

I move my unwilling body further back onto my thin-mattressed bed in order to lean against the cool, concrete wall. Eyes wide open I look around the room which they think is my prison. I have been labeled demente, loco.

"She's so bobo!" the women in white uniforms whisper to each other.

They think I don't hear them? They are demente! They know nothing! This room is not my prison. It is true I am a prisoner but my jail cell sits like an enemy soldier atop my shoulders. My mind is a detention centre. My heart is a penitentiary. I am serving a life sentence and there is no escape for one such as me.

Write it down.

I hold the pen steady with my right hand. I stare at my hand and watch it as it begins to move across the line on the page leaving behind it little scrawls which are trying to be doorways to sanity. I am fascinated by these scrawls. They look like they are trying to be words. My hand is holding the pen but I am not the author.

I know I am not worthy to be dead, to live in paradise with my Gabriela. God has no use for me. So who is it that is scribbling and making these dark marks on the page? Is this the work of the devil himself? No, it is the crazy woman writing in the book. I should not read what is written. But why not? I am already cursed, aren't I?   Is it possible that if I follow the sentences they will lead me out of darkness into light?

But there is no one to answer my questions. Where are you, Father? Why aren't you here with me?

I am detached from the crazy woman who did the unforgivable. Her words can't hurt me.   I begin to read the words that the hand of the lunatic is writing.

My name is Eva Soto. I was born 24 years ago in a city named Talcahuano.   In the classroom I learned that the meaning of Talcahuano is thundering sky. My city is in the Province of Concepcion in the country of Chile.   I am only one inhabitant of this big city which has a population of more than 250,000 citizens.

A large percentage of the residents of Talcahuano share my ancestry which is Aymara. The Aymara people are a very proud race and even today in

14

2010 we still follow many practices which are an integral part of our ancient Maya culture.

As a young child I learned of the Maya prophecy which promised that a huge wave will end our world as we know it. At the time I first heard these words I thought the prophecy was no more than a fairy tale; a made-up story like Bartolo and his bird cages. Bartolo was a young man from a poor background who desired to raise his status in the world by marrying the daughter of the Lord of the Castle. To win her hand he gave to her father a blue bird, belief in which would give him all the gold and riches one could imagine.

But when the Lord of the Castle accepted the blue bird in exchange for his daughter he was astonished to find that it was just a large, gray bird which glared at him in a very rude way before he escaped his cage and flew out the window. The *promise of the huge wave was as false as the promise of the blue bird.*

And how was I, Eva Soto, any different from the young Bartolo? My parents are simple peasants who are raising too many children in a crowded house in a poor Talcahuano barrio. Like our neighbours we are Roman Catholic and, as such, we attend church and believe the priest who tells us we must be married and have many children. And we must do these things in an orderly way. Marriage must come before children. We are warned.

I don't listen to the warnings of the church or the warnings of my mother anymore than I pay attention to the warnings of the Mayan Prophecy of a huge wave. I am the oldest of my parents' children and just like Bartolo I dream of an easier life away from the dreariness of painful poverty.

The day I meet Robert I believe my dreams have come true.

Robert? Who is writing about Robert? I cannot believe what I am reading. I cannot allow another to write about things when no one, no one but me, knows the truth.

This realization shocks me into becoming myself. I remember I didn't want to be me anymore. I didn't want to live. But now after reading the words written by the lunatic I know I must take charge. No one else can tell my story. This is not a risk I am willing to take. As I begin to feel the presence of the pen in my right hand I realize it wants to move of its own accord. I will not allow that to continue. No, it is my story and mine to tell.

Already the crazy woman has filled the lines on several pages in the violet covered book. I read them all over once again and when I am finished I am surprised but satisfied to see that all that the insane person has written is true. I wonder how this disordered, deranged person knows so much about me. I know nothing about her and I don't want to know anything about her. I am glad she has left and I hope she never comes back. How dare she write my name and pretend that she is me?

I begin to write. And I commence where she left off.

The day I meet Robert I believe my dreams have come true. I am seventeen years old. He is a handsome, young Canadian who is living with his family in Chile. He is tall, fair complexioned and his eyes are a soft shade of violet. "No one has violet eyes," I insist.

"You are wrong," Robert answers. "Elizabeth Taylor has violet eyes and so does my mother and, as you can see, so do I."

Robert loves me and he promises he will take me with him back to Canada when his family returns at the end of the year. He promises he will love me forever and he shows me that it is not so very difficult to transform a seventeen year old girl into a woman.

My mother warns me to stay with my own kind. I don't want to listen to her. I have no desire to continue the cycle of poverty and superstition that reigns over our barrio.

When I discover that I am expecting a baby I tell Robert. I want to share my joy. I know he will feel as proud as I do and together we will be loving parents to our child in rich, clean Canada.

One day I knock on the door of Robert's parents' home. There is no answer. For many weeks I return to knock on that door. I don't want to believe the old cleaning lady when she tells me that the family has moved back to Canada. "They are gone, I tell you," she insists. "I am cleaning this house to prepare it for the new tenants."

My Gabriela is born. For seven years we live in my parents' crowded house. With reluctance my mother looks after my child while I work in a better part of town as a domestic in a rich home.

I am in bed asleep when it happens. At first the house shakes in frenzy. My ears are deafened by the loud roaring of what sounds like a train overhead. The earth dances a crazy reel and my life turns upside down. I don't know it is an earthquake. I only know I must get to my Gabriela who sleeps with my younger brothers and sisters in the room next to mine.

I jump out of bed and when my feet hit the floor I start to run but something whacks the side of my head. I fall to the ground.

I gain consciousness when the water begins to lap at my brain. I awake and realize the house is filling with water. Where is the water coming from? I have no idea. But the water level is rising too fast. I call out to my parents but hear no reply.

"Gabriela!"

The water is above my waist now. I need to get to my daughter. I begin to swim and when I reach her room I see her holding on for dear life atop the high wardrobe. She is my beautiful seven-year-old baby.

"Mama!" she cries. "Help me, Mama!"

"Hang on, Gabriela. I'm coming. Hang on!" I shout.

It was then I hear the explosion. The house is torn apart. I am thrown and land on the roof. Somehow I climb from the roof to a tree which I begin to climb.

From this high vantage point my eyes dare to look downward. My Gabriela is gone. She is nowhere to be seen. I stare at the dirty water below me. I know where my baby is when bubbles rise.

"Let me die too, God,"

God remains silent.

"Why won't anyone listen to me?" I scream aloud.

Father Morales speaks "I hear you, Eva"

I stop writing. At last, I can cry.

THE FACE IN THE MIRROR

His motorcycle was a mess after the night's big rumble, but Randy didn't let that stop him. He'd get out of town fast. He hopped onto his bike and drove away intending never to come back until he turned his bleeding head and saw his face in the bike's mangled mirror.

Was it pure happenstance that the frightening imagery stopped him in his tracks or was there something more mystical, more powerful at work? At once Randy remembered his mother, Maria.   He pulled the damaged bike over to the city street's concrete curb then bent his tall, too thin, wiry body over to get a closer look in the mirror at his lacerated forehead. He didn't like what he saw. The broken glass showed a reflection of the young man's broken dreams. Then Randy did something he thought he would never do.

He cried.

Leaving his busted bike at the curb he began to wearily wander along the uncaring sidewalk filled with city-stressed pedestrians going here, going there. Randy was going nowhere. Head bowed low he walked toward the walk-up apartment he used to call home. He couldn't call it that anymore now that Maria was gone. She was his home and without her he was nobody. He was nobody going nowhere. His tears mingled with the blood. Randy raised his left arm and swiped at the side of his forlorn face.   Staring at the blood stains on his torn leather jacket sleeve he began to cry like a baby. Ma, I'm so tired. Mama, help me, he prayed.

At last he turned the corner onto his street. There wasn't much time. The street was quiet with no one about but just to be sure Randy looked over his shoulder to be certain he wasn't being followed before he entered his building. He climbed the narrow steel stairway and entered the third floor apartment. He headed straight for the bathroom. Grabbing a towel from the rack he ran the cold water tap over it and held it up to his throbbing forehead to absorb the blood. He looked at his world- weary face in the mirror. Suddenly the beautiful Maria was there. She stood beside him and Randy was seventeen again.

"Randolpho!" she shouted. "Randolpho, you like what you see in that mirror?"

"Leave me be, ma. Stop your worrying."

"Ha! Big man Randolpho! Skipping school! Running with that gang of no-good bums! This is what you want for your life?   You think this is what I want

for you?   You like what you see in that mirror?   What

kind of example are you setting for your brother,

Jimmy? "

"Lay off, ma! Leave me be. Trust me; I know

what I'm doing."

"Ha! Trust! I put my trust in God. For you, I

pray, my son. I'm scared for you. I beg you,

Randolpho, stop running with that gang of no-good

hoodlums."

Now three years later was Randy finally ready

to listen to his mother?

Maria had been murdered by rival gang

members just three months ago in a drive-by shooting.

She was on her way home from working the evening

shift at the local bar and grill where she waitressed.

Randy waved when he saw her coming down the street

and hurried toward her to help carry the grocery bags she was struggling with in her hands. He stood there, paralyzed, as his dear mother's body crumpled to the sidewalk less than a foot away from him. He knew the bullets were meant for him. He swore vengeance.

He didn't know how many were slaughtered in the rumble tonight. His gang was victorious but it was a hollow victory. Yeah, we won, Randy acknowledged, but as he stared at himself in the smudgy bathroom mirror he could only question with bewilderment what was won. Where's the prize, he wondered. And staring into his pain-filled eyes he had to admit, "I'm no prize. You were right, ma! I hate what I see in the mirror. Help me, ma! I don't know what to do."

He removed the cold wet cloth from his injured head. The bleeding finally stopped. He patched up the worst of the cuts with a myriad of Band-Aids then left the bathroom and walked to the kitchen at the back of the silent apartment. The green glass vase was still sitting atop the soiled, yellow flowered oilcloth that covered the old wooden kitchen table. Randy sat down at the table and staring at the vase he remembered how his mother always kept it filled with water and fresh cut flowers from the corner market. Today the vase was dry, water-stained, and held nothing but a bunch of wilted red and white carnations and one single droopy, dead daisy.

Enough! Randy rose from the kitchen chair, lifted the vase and carried it over to the counter. He trashed the dead flowers. He searched under the sink and retrieved an SOS pad from an opened box. Turning on the tap he let the water run until it was hot at last. Then he scoured the vase until it was clear and clean. He grabbed the dishcloth and with gave the oilcloth a good wipe. He kept at it until the stains were almost gone.   Then he placed the empty vase back into the centre of the table. Without the flowers the vase looked as little and lonely as Randy felt.

What to do? What to do, he wondered.   He knew the rival gang would seek reprisal. There was no doubt about that. He went into his bedroom, pulled down his old backpack and started stuffing it with some of his jeans and shirts. He'd get out of town but where would he go?

And then he heard him. "Randy, is that you, Randy?"

Jimmy! He'd forgotten all about Jimmy!   His mother was right about him.   She had him pegged. What kind of a useless turd forgets his little brother?

Then twelve year old Jimmy was there in his bedroom.   "What are ya doin', Randy? Why you packin' up? You going somewhere? I'm comin' with

ya, right? Where we goin', Randy? "

With reluctance Randy turned to face his little

brother. Seeing the bandages on his forehead, Jimmy

was scared. He asked, "What's happened to ya,

Randy?"

"A rumble tonight, Jimmy. I can't waste any

time. I gotta get out of town for a while."

"Let me join the gang, Randy. I'm old enough.

I can help you fight."

Randy heard his little brother's plea but louder

than that he heard the desperation in Maria's voice as

she asked, "What kind of example are you setting for

your brother, Jimmy?"

Randy stared at Jimmy. He saw a good-looking

kid with blue eyes and blond hair. Looking closer he

saw a motherless child; a city kid who would be a gangster in no time at all if Randy didn't wake up and do something about their hopeless situation. Looking even closer he saw himself as he had been eight years ago; innocent, hopeful, and optimistic. But in those days he had a family. That was before his father Giuseppe had the massive heart attack and died; before his beautiful mother, Maria, had to spend all her time waitressing at the local bar and grill to keep food on the table for her stalwart sons.

With helplessness Randy looked at his little brother and felt overcome by realization. I'm the only family Jimmy's got in this godforsaken world. Help me, ma! I don't know what to do.

"Come here, kid," Randy said. He held out his arms and Jimmy walked into his big brother's warm embrace. "You're the only family I've got now, Jimmy. Don't you worry. I'll take care of ya. I've got to figure out what to do." Releasing his brother Randy allowed his eyes to roam the room seeking the well hidden answer that refused to reveal itself.

Jimmy followed his big brother back into the kitchen where Randy put on a pot of coffee. While they waited for their drinks they sat across from each other at the kitchen table. When the room was filled with the aroma of strong coffee Randy got up from the table and reached into the cupboard for a couple of mugs. He filled the cups with coffee. He plunked the hot cups onto the table then with greater care set one in front of his brother. "Here kid, drink this."

"I'm hungry, Randy."

"I know you are, kid. Don't worry. We'll get something to eat later."

Randy was about to sit down at the table across from Jimmy when his eyes landed on an old photo that sat on a little shelf beside the condiments over the old kitchen gas stove. Randy lifted the framed photo off the shelf and showed it to his little brother. "Look at this, Jimmy," he said. "You know who these people are, kid?"

"Sure," Jimmy answered. "That's ma."

"I know that's ma, Jimmy. But who's that in the picture with ma?"

"I don't know who the guy is, Randy."

"Well, do you know the woman? She looks familiar. Who's the woman, Jimmy?"

"I'm not sure but I think that's ma's sister, Rosalie."

"Rosalie," Randy repeated. "Sure, I remember ma talking about her sister, Rosalie. Seems to me I remember hearing that she lives with her family in a little town a few hours outside the city. If I'm not mistaken she lives pretty far north of here."

"Did we ever meet her, Randy?"

"As far as I know we never met her, Jimmy, at least not that I can remember, but I know ma used to sometimes talk to her on the phone, eh?"

"Yeah, that's right, Randy. I remember that too."

"I can't remember the name of the guy Rosalie married. Guess you don't know either, eh?"

"Nope."

"Jimmy, do you remember where ma kept her little phone book?"

"No, I don't, but it's probably somewhere in one of her bedroom dresser drawers or maybe even in her purse."

The two boys forgot all about drinking their coffee. Instead they searched until they found Rosalie's phone number.   Randy dialed and spoke for the first time with his Aunt Rosalie.   When he hung up the phone he gazed into Jimmy's hopeful, enquiring eyes. "Start packing, Jimmy. We're leaving this city and we are moving north."

"Aunt Rosalie gonna take us in, Randy?"

"Yep. We are going to start over with a clean slate, Jimmy. No bikes, no gangs and no violence. We're gonna make ma proud, you and me.   So start packing Jimmy!"

"Where we going, Randy? Where does Aunt Rosalie live?"

"Some little town up north called Elliot Lake, Jimmy. She said she was working as an aide or a nurse of some kind in an old age nursing home up there."

The boys were just about ready to leave. Randy checked his wallet to make sure he had enough money for their bus fare. Rosalie would meet them at the other end and drive them to the home that she shared with her school teacher husband and their three children. The brothers would be part of a family once again.

Randy was finishing up in the little bathroom. He had tidied up his forehead as best he could and replaced the band aids with one bandage in a tidier fashion. He wanted to make as good an impression on his aunt as he possibly could. He looked into the mirror over the sink. Again Maria was there. Again he remembered her asking, "Randolpho, you like what you see in that mirror?"

"I'm trying, ma. I'm gonna do my best, I promise."

Before he left the bathroom Randy could have sworn he heard his mother's voice. "I like. I like what I see in that mirror, son."

"Ready to go, Jimmy?" he shouted.

"All set, Randy!"

Randy locked the apartment door and tossed the key into a trash can in the hallway. He wouldn't need it again. They would not be back.

CHANTI'S ESCAPE

My name is Chanti. Today I am old but at the time of my birth the light in my father's deep brown eyes shone bright enough to light all the homes in Nawada. My mother, Aadita, was a puzzle to me for most of my childhood years. You might even say she was tsundere. She would say mean things to my father Mahavir yet as I grew older I began to realize that behind my mother's cutting remarks lay a warm heart. For her own reasons my mother kept her softer side hidden. Perhaps this was the way she chose to protect herself from the harsh realities of life in the small town of Nawada where we lived.

The name Aadita means *from the beginning*. But my mother's true personality was not always evident to an observer's eyes at first meeting. One might even think she is hostile however the longer one knew my mother the more obvious it became that she had a soft heart.

By the time I was seven I would carry the bucket to the public water tap. Clean water was not always readily available. If we were lucky we would have water on alternate days but most often the tap would be running once a week. On the days when water was available I would fill the bucket and carry it back to our home.

If I spilled even a drop of water my mother would shout, "Stupid child! Stupid child, watch what you are doing!"

My father had a softer side and he would always step in to protect me from my mother's wicked tongue lashing. His name Mahavir, I came to learn, meant *great hero* and throughout my childhood and even longer my father was just that to me.

My earliest memories of my home town of Nawada are vague. Nawada is located in the larger area of South Bihar in India. The residents of Nawada live on both sides of the River Khuri. The right bank was more modern and it was there that one would see government buildings, manufacturing plants and other important places.   We lived on the left bank; the older part of town and it was here that one would see pitted roads, piles of garbage, open drains and stagnant pools of water.

In Nawada an observer would see many street urchins. Child labour was customary but not all children were fortunate to have a job. I was more fortunate than most of the other children in South Bihar. I was neither a child labourer nor a street urchin. My father who worked as a potter provided well for my mother and for me, his only child. My name Chanti means *peace* and, apart from my mother's sporadic ranting and ravings, it was with peace that my childhood years were filled. No one ever laid a hand on me in anger.

My parents are Hindu. They named me Chanti not only because the name denotes peace but also because Chanti is the vocal ending to an Upanishad. Upanishads are philosophical texts that form the basis of my parents' Hindu religion. These texts are also known as Vedanta. My father was a religious man. When he was not working as a potter creating the ornamental pottery in the manufacturing plant on the right bank of the River Khuri, he was in the temple where he studied and prayed. Although a poor man, my father Mahavir Kumhar was a rich man with a wealth of knowledge.

My mother, like most women in Nawada, was uneducated. Her mother, my grandmother, Abishta meaning *lady of the house* was exactly that. She was expert in the art of cooking, sewing and all aspects of keeping a house in order. It was my grandmother who taught my mother and it is my mother who teaches me the most important duties of a Hindu woman in South Bihar, India. Hindu women are taught to serve their husbands and their families. Their own desires are of lesser importance and they are buried under the daily tasks. Perhaps it is this very burial that causes my mother to be tsundere.

And this was my upbringing. I was ordered about by my mother and I was pampered by my father who would often read to me and teach me to always have reverence and respect for the Hindu faith. My father would often speak to me of other countries in the world; especially America. He would tell me that in

America the streets are paved with diamonds and that everyone is rich. Americans, he would say, have clean water every day and electric light that is constant and reliable.

"Would you like to live in America?" I once asked him.

"And who would not like to live in such a wonderful place?" was his response.

My father knew of Americans because the people who owned the pottery plant where he worked were from America. Yes, they were Indian but they were people who had immigrated to America and, indeed, some of these people were actually born in America.

As I grew older I recall my father telling me that sometimes these American Indians returned to South Bihar and to Nawada in particular to find a good wife.

These fortunate women who made a good impression upon the Americans would marry and they would then travel to America with their new husbands where they would make their home in comfort and richness. My father told me that when I reached a marriageable age he would do his utmost to achieve this type of union for me.

I dreamed of such a rich life when I carried the bucket of water from the public tap to our home. I dreamed of such a rich life when I bent to sweep the floor or got down on my knees to clean my father's shoes.

That day arrived sooner than I had imagined. It was on the occasion of my thirteenth birthday that my father arrived home from his work as a potter. With him was a man whose face gleamed. Never had I seen such a complexion. His face was white yet pink yet brown with spots that I later learned were called freckles. A freckle was never found on the brown face of an Indian. It was laughable yet it was intriguing in its difference, in its uniqueness.

My mother was much more subservient than usual when my father brought this man into our humble home. She bowed and she scurried about to place the bowls of food onto our table. "This way, child," she would admonish me when I failed to quickly respond to her requests. Neither of my parents had prepared me for this special meal yet it was obvious to me that my mother outdid herself in the preparation of this dining experience with the white man from America.

My mother adhered strictly to Bihari cuisine. Usually vegetarian in our daily fare my mother made an exception to this rule to please our American visitor. I carried the bowl of steaming fish curry to the table. I also ladled the Sattu Paratha onto the banana leaves. Sattu Paratha was Parathas stuffed with fried chickpea flour. I had helped my mother to prepare this recipe. On this special day my mother also served Chokha which consists of spicy mashed potatoes. This meal was indeed a feast.

Little did I know that it was to be almost my last meal as an innocent little girl; daughter of my parents. This feast was my introduction to Sam, an American who I soon learned was a Canadian. During this meal I also learned that my life in Nawada, South Bihar, India would soon be traded for a life on rich Canadian soil.

That evening we sat at the table, my father, my mother, Sam Saraswati and me. My parents and I had excellent table manners eating as we did with our hands. It was impossible not to notice the awkwardness of the Canadian stranger. "Forgive me," he said in perfect English, "I am not accustomed to eating with my hands. In Elliot Lake, Ontario, where I live in Canada it is the custom to use utensils, knives, forks and spoons, when we eat our meals."

I had no understanding of his apology. I knew no other way of eating. Always in our home we ate with our hands. I wanted to ask, "What is a fork?" What is a knife? But I did not want to show my ignorance. Besides it was unseemly that a female child of thirteen should question the words of an adult, especially one who was foreign.

Of course I had heard my father talk about the white Americans but never before had I seen one with my own eyes. During that dinner I learned that I was to be the bride of Sam Saraswati. I also learned that there would be a wedding feast within two weeks, after which I would travel with my new husband to my new home in Elliot Lake, Canada.

To describe my feelings at that time is impossible. Everything being told to me seemed no more than a mystery. To leave my parents was a terrifying prospect. At the same time to live in a place where the streets are paved with diamonds and where everyone is rich was an intriguing and exciting invitation. How could I not want such a rewarding and comfortable life?

Throughout this feast I said nothing. My mother said very little. My father and the Canadian did all of the talking; mostly Sam Saraswati.
"How is it that an Indian man has such fair skin?" my father enquired.

Sam had no hesitation in his reply. "My grandfather was born in Nawada. He travelled as a young man to Canada where he married a white Christian woman. Their son, my father was a mixture of brown and white and his complexion was probably

48

best described as olive. My father adopted and lived the Hindu principles of his father before him. However like my grandfather, he also married a white Christian woman who had red hair and a freckled face. I am the result of this pairing.   I was born in Canada and I am a Canadian citizen. Physically I am a white man but in my heart I am a very proud Indian and I adhere to the faith and the principles of my Hindu forefathers."

"And you wish to marry an Indian woman?" my father asked.

"Indeed, I do, sir," Sam responded. "I find your daughter beautiful."

I lowered my eyes when I heard him say these words. Embarrassed, I stopped eating. No one had called me beautiful before; not even my father who loved me and certainly never my mother who would not waste her words on unnecessary compliments.

When the feast was ended my father and Sam Saraswati moved out of our front room to the verandah where they continued to talk. I stayed in the house with my mother. Together we cleared the table and began the task of cleaning the plates and the bowls.

For the first time in my entire life I saw a tear in my mother's eye as she said, "You will marry this man. You will leave our home and travel to Canada."

"No, mommy, no," I cried.

"Yes, child. The agreement has been made. Stop your crying. We have no time to waste on tears."

I did see that tear in my mother's eye. Yes, I did.

At the age of thirteen I married this white man, Sam Saraswati. Ours was a traditional Hindu ceremony which took place in the Nawadi Temple. When I entered the priest was reciting *slokas* filling the temple with positive energy. I took my place beside Sam Saraswati and we exchanged flower garlands. My parents placed my hand into the white freckled hand of the stranger.

All the traditional rituals were carried out and soon it was time for the groom and for me to take the seven steps which we did and soon I heard myself repeating the seventh step, *"Let us take the seventh step to stay best friends in this lifelong wedlock."* I looked into the face of Sam Saraswati and wondered how this white stranger could ever be my best friend. I barely knew him.

But then it was time. Sam and I received blessings from my parents and from his parents whom I had met only hours before the ceremony. We touched their feet. This is called the Aushirwad. The rituals and vows were complete. It seemed impossibility to me but I had to accept that I was now a married woman.

Saying good-bye to my parents was a painful experience. Stepping into the airliner that would take me to Canada was more excitement than I could bear.

I arrived with Sam and his parents in a huge airport in Toronto. From Toronto we travelled for hours by bus until we reached the small town of Elliot Lake. I was disappointed. The streets were not lined with diamonds. It was winter and the streets were lined with dirty snow banks. The roads were slushy and slippery. Before leaving South Bihar I had never seen snow nor had I ever felt such cold temperatures.

The bus pulled into place at a small station. Sam and his father carried our belongings while I walked with his mother who guided me to a parked vehicle. She directed me to get into the back seat which I did. She climbed in also and sat beside me. Sam and his father sat in the front seat. Sam drove the car but it was a very short trip. Before I barely had a chance to look around at my new surroundings he was pulling the car into the driveway of a small bungalow that was painted white and boasted black shutters on the windows.

My first impression of the house was that it was a nice home but certainly it was far from the luxury and the richness I had heard about and expected from this bountiful America. Sam and I moved into his parents' house and on this day I became the servant to this red-headed white woman who dressed like a man in pants and shirts that she called blouses. My beautiful saris were hung in a closet and Shirley Saraswati provided me with clothing that was very similar to her own but, of course, in a smaller size as I was only thirteen and my breasts had barely begun to present themselves.

In time I learned to like my mother-in-law. She was kind to me and she taught me the ways of the western world. In the first few months of my Canadian residence I began to enjoy my life in spite of the fact that I dearly missed my parents; especially my daddy who treated me like his little princess. Sam did not treat me like a princess. For the most part he ignored me as he went about his business which I knew next to nothing about. He made frequent trips to India in his line of duties but not once did he invite me to accompany him that I might visit with my parents.

Everything changed when Mr. and Mrs. Saraswati died. They were not old people by any means and their death came as a shock to Sam and to me. They had gone out in their car to do a little shopping. Weather was poor and they were involved in an accident on Highway 108. Both were severely injured and both died later in hospital.

By then I was fifteen years of age. By Canadian standards I was just a kid, a teenager. But by Indian standards I was a woman married for two years. I was now the matron, the keeper of the house and it was my duty to take over all the tasks that had previously been performed by Shirley Saraswati.

I did my best to keep a tidy home. I shopped. I cooked. I did the laundry. I looked after the needs of my husband and they were many and I soon learned that they were strange; particularly his needs in the bedroom. Of course I had no experience. I had no education in matters of this kind but even today as I recall my life with Sam I know that his needs were far from normal.

To say that he was rough with me is putting it mildly. It gave him pleasure to dominate me into submission. This domination carried over into our daily lives. I was like his indentured servant. I knew nothing else. My Canadian dream was a nightmare. I was trapped.

I tried to make the best of this new life of mine. I never ever grew to like the large white body that hovered over me and pushed its way into my peace of mind. Never!

I gave birth to two children; two boys neither of whom were dark skinned like me. Neither were they white like their father. My children were beautiful and they were well-behaved.   They attended school and being smart like their father they moved away from home once they completed high school and they were enrolled in university.

Once the children were out of the home and it was just Sam and me once again, Sam grew even rougher in his behaviour toward me.   His abuse was no longer limited to the bedroom. It was not uncommon for him to slap me if he did not like the way I prepared his evening meal. He would punch me if I did not clean the house as well as he deemed it should be done.   He called me names like whore and slut. Yet there was nothing in my life that would give credence to these disgusting names. I left the house only to shop. In all my years living in Elliot Lake I never felt like a Canadian woman. I was my husband's servant.

When the children were still quite young I began to save money from the grocery allowance Sam granted me each week. I couldn't save much because if I did he would be sure to notice. But each week I was able to put aside a few dollars. For years I saved in this way; not in a Canadian bank. Oh, no, not at all. I saved this money in a small cloth bag which I kept hidden within one of my saris that never in all the years made their way out of that bedroom closet.

Sam's abuse increased over the years; it increased faster than my savings. I made a promise to myself that my day would come. My day when I would leave this house, leave Sam, leave this country and return to Nawada would indeed take place.

My sons graduated from university. One is a lawyer and the other is a pharmacist. They married and they both married white Canadian girls. I have grandchildren who have never been given the opportunity to meet their dark skinned Indian grandmother. I have only photos of these children. Sam visits Toronto and he spends time with his sons and the grandchildren but Sam forbids me to accompany him. Just like in the early days of our marriage he more or less ignores me and carries on his life as though I didn't exist; except of course when he is in need of someone to abuse, to push around, to punish.

I have often thought of leaving Sam; often, some days it is all I can think about. Sometimes I think Sam can read my mind because more than once he has said, "If you ever try to leave me I will kill you. Do you understand? I will kill you and you will not even be missed by anyone."

I had no reason not to believe what he said. I knew he would carry through on his murderous threats. Sam was a dangerous man. Getting away from him would not be easy. But still I continued to save. My money transformed from hundreds to thousands. I believe I finally have enough money in order to escape this prison.

But in all these years I've grown old. My parents have died and I did not even have the privilege of visiting Nawada to attend their burial service. Yes, Sam attended on my behalf. Like my mother before me I hid my tears. Like my mother before me I have become *tsundere*. I have a warm heart but I keep my heart in my pocket. I share it with no one; not even my sons who obey their father and refuse to visit their mother.

Now too many years have gone by. My children are now grandparents. I have great grandchildren that I have never met. Yes, I have seen photos that Sam, in his graciousness, has occasionally allowed me to view.

I am sixty-eight years old. For fifty-five years I have remained in this house which is just a little older than me. My money remains safe in my sari. I believe I may soon die. I know that if I do not act soon I will fail to keep the promise I made to myself many years ago.

I have been dead inside for so many years that one would think I had grown immune to Sam's threats of death. But they do bother me; they are a bane to my existence. One might label me a coward and certainly a fool to have remained in a loveless marriage throughout my entire life. I try to forgive myself for my cowardice; for my lack of action; for my low self-esteem.

I try but I fail to excuse myself.

I awoke one morning last week. It was mid-November. Diwali was over. The Festival of Lights was never much of a celebration in the Saraswati family. Most years it was a day like any other and this year was no exception.   But Diwali was a reminder to me to let the light within me shine. I wondered if that light still existed; the light that shone when I was privileged to be my daddy's little princess and my mother's dutiful daughter.

When I awoke one morning last week I thought about the night before when Sam, caught up in his sick desire, had slapped me until my body was bruised. As he hit me he declared his love for me. I was used to his perverted ways. I was used to being treated like an object that was less than human.

Even in his old age Sam continues to abuse me just as he continues to threaten me just as he believes his behaviour is an expression of love. I was sixty-eight years old. I may not have many years left. Sam's sick twisted passion of the night before was the last straw. It's time to put an end to the madness. It is time to let my light shine. I must do this. I must have some peace before my life on earth comes to an end.

My decision was made. When I awoke that morning I began to make my list. I wrote down the words *People to say good-bye* to. Then just as quickly I crossed that off my list. Who would I say goodbye to?

My children? My grandchildren?   They were strangers to me. I had no friends. There was no one in the entire world to whom I needed to say good-bye.

And then I wondered once I run away, where will I go? To whom will I say hello? Who wants to be bothered with the old woman that I have become?

I continued with my list: *stuff to pack,* and that would be just my clothes and maybe the photos of my children and my grandchildren. Certainly I will pack my saris. I hoped and I believed that at least one day before I die I will once more wear my saris and walk with pride among my own people.

To my list I added *bus tickets; plane tickets.* Even getting to the bus station presented a problem since Sam never allowed me to drive a car. To my list I added *call a taxi.* I didn't bother adding *things to get rid of* to my list. That would make the list ten miles long. The most important thing I would get rid of is my detention, my imprisonment.

For once I will be free. For the first time in my long life I will taste freedom.

The day arrived at last. I have the tickets in my possession. I've packed my clothes and kept my suitcases hidden beneath the bed. I am ready to go. I have memorized the phone number for the taxi. I pick up the receiver to dial when the front door of the house opens and Sam comes into the house. It is the middle of the day and Sam is never at home in the middle of the day. I am cursed. I am plagued.

"What did I tell you I would do if you ever tried to leave me, Chanti?"

I stood, telephone in hand, facing him, frozen, paralyzed.

"Answer me woman! What did I tell you I would do?"

"You said you would kill me," I whispered.

"Are you ready to die?" he demanded.

From somewhere deep within me something strange, something totally unknown began to rise. I could feel it though I could not name it. I allowed it to surface and when it did the words jumped from my mouth. "I have been dead for fifty-five years. Today I am ready to live."

Angered by my words he strode across the room. He grabbed the telephone receiver out of my hand. He raised it and just as he was about to land it upon the top of my head I reached out my hand and I grabbed the sewing scissors from the table upon which the telephone rested.

The receiver swung down. I crouched and scissors in hand I plunged. They met their target. The telephone receiver fell to the floor beside me. Sam fell to the floor in front of me.

For just a moment I allowed myself to wonder how long it would be before someone unknown to me would miss Sam; would come looking for him. I knew I had to hurry. I picked up the receiver, dialed the memorized taxi number. I stepped over his body and from my bedroom I pulled my suitcases out from under the bed. I put on my winter coat and swung my handbag over my shoulder; the precious handbag that held the bus ticket, the plane ticket, the passport, the cloth bag filled with money that I had been saving for more than fifty years.

My name is Chanti. Today I am old but at the time of my birth the light in my father's deep brown eyes shone bright enough to light all the homes in

Nawada. Today, at long last, that very light shines in my own eyes and it lights the path before me. I will follow this light and make my escape. It is time.

UNDER THE HUMMINGTREE

I know I am not supposed to play favourites but my grandson, Lucien, is the kind of boy who melts my heart. I've always thought he's a bit slow in the head. I've said as much to his mother but she doesn't pay attention to anything I have to say in the best of times.

My Lucien has had more than his fair share of troubles in his short life but the day that stands out in my mind is that Tuesday six years ago when Lucien was only ten.

"He's a bit slow in the head," I said to my daughter again that morning.

"Learning difficulties, Mom! He has learning difficulties!"

"I know, Carol. That's what I'm saying. He's a bit slow in the head but he's a good boy."

"I give up!" my daughter shouted. "Lucien has enough trouble getting by at school without you telling him he's a bit slow in the head!"

"I never said any such thing to him, Carol. It's you I'm talking to."

"I've gotta go, Mom or I'll be late for work. Make sure Lucien gets to school on time!"

Carol was out the door before I had a chance to answer. Why she thinks she needs to remind me to get Lucien to school on time is beyond me. I've been doing it now for five years ever since Peter took off leaving Carol to raise Lucien on her own. Lucien was only five years old when his deadbeat dad up and left.

I helped out as much as I could and at fifty-seven I was doing my best but barely managed on my fixed income. When Carol came to me and asked if I would take care of Lucien while she went out to work I couldn't say no. My daughter wanted my help. I knew she had no one else she could leave Lucien with so how could I say no?

Though I had raised my two girls on my own, I just didn't feel confident about my role in the raising of Lucien. It was hard to put my finger on what it was that made Lucien different from other children his age. Innocence swallowed him. Unlike the other kids in the neighbourhood he was not street smart. From the earliest age he was a loner. He didn't seem to know how to give a flip answer to the taunts that came his way. He was always the butt of the joke. He kept to himself and tried to steer clear of trouble but he was a target to the other kids. Keeping my eye on him didn't stop the teasing taunts that shadowed him every day on his lonely journey to and from school.

Carol would drop Lucien off at my house at seven a.m. each morning on her way to work. There were times when I felt that the challenges of raising this boy were too much for a woman my age. At those times I would go into my backyard and sit on God's good earth beneath the branches of my Hummingtree. I would share my thoughts and fears with my anchor who lived in the yellow quartz rock at the foot of the Lilac.

"Not so sure I can manage the raising of this boy," I would say.

And the comforting voice would reply, "Remember there is only one path. You've been alone too long. Raising Lucien will lift your head out of the sand. You will find new purpose in life. Ellen, the boy needs you."

"Needs me? What Lucien needs is a stable home with a father who is present and a mother who isn't too tired to listen."

"The boy needs you, Ellen," the voice repeated.

"The boy's got me," I said. "I'm doing my best and I just hope it is good enough."

When Lucien was five I used to walk the two blocks down the road to the school with him. A beautiful boy with his blue eyes and curly brown hair, he would hold tight to my hand and say, "Gram, I don't want to go to school."

"You have to go to school, Lucien," I would tell him.

"The kids laugh at me, Gram. I don't want to go to school," he would insist.

"You have to go to school, Lucien. Why are the kids laughing at you?"

"I don't know, Gram. But they do and I don't like it."

When Carol came home from work that night I told her what Lucien had said.

"Why are they laughing at him, Mom?" she asked me.

"I don't know, Carol. He's a good boy but I think he's a little slow in the head. Kids can be cruel! You know that."

"I'll talk to his teacher," she said. And that was the end of that.

By the time Lucien was eight years old he didn't want me to walk to school with him anymore. "It's just down the street, Gram. I can go by myself. The kids tease me. They call me a little baby 'cause I'm walking to school with my grandma."

I didn't want to but I knew I had to loosen my grip. I had no choice. I had to stop walking with him to school.

My new habit was to send him off to school on his own. Then I'd grab my bundle buggy and pull it along behind me as I walked. I'd keep my distance behind him but my eye was always on Lucien until he turned into the school yard. Then I'd carry on up the street, turn at the corner and go into the Dominion Store to do some shopping. I did that every morning for several months. Those days I always had more food in the house than I knew what to do with.

Throughout the spring and summer I would make a point of doing my front yard gardening at the time when school was letting out for the day. Before watering the flowers I would do my weeding. Then I would take my trowel and loosen the earth around the rose bush and the peony plants. By the time I was standing there, hose in hand, watering the garden, school would be out and the children would be coming down the street on their way home.

Throughout the winter months I would time it just right in order to be in the driveway clearing away the snow when the school bell sounded.

I didn't have the cataracts then as I do now and my vision was just about okay. I could spot Lucien coming along down the sidewalk by the time he was a little more than a block away. I couldn't help noticing that while other children walked together in groups of two or three, Lucien would always be walking home from school by himself. While other children would be shouting and laughing, Lucien would walk head down in silence.

The temptation to turn off the water, put the hose aside and get out there to walk with my grandson was always with me. But I resisted the urge and stayed where I was. The other kids already thought he was a sissy and I didn't want to make things any worse for him than they already were. He never knew I was watching him in this way. No one knew. This was something I shared only with my rock beneath the Hummingtree.

In this way I was able to offer some protection to Lucien on his way to and from school. Of course I had no control over what took place in the schoolyard before classes started or during recess. I know he was teased. Lucien was a simple, trusting child and he would share with me in his own matter-of-fact way.

"They called me an idiot today, Gram."

"Who called you an idiot, Lucien?" I asked.

"The other kids. They called me an idiot 'cause they said I got nobody home upstairs. How come they say these things to me, Gram? We don't even have an upstairs in this house."

"Don't you pay one bit of attention to what those kids say to you, Lucien!"

I wanted to beat the tar out of those little brats. I wanted to teach them a lesson or two but my hands were tied. I hated to worry her but I did tell Carol about it. I felt like I had to.

"I'll talk to his teacher," was all she would ever say to me about it.

The years went by in much the same way. I wanted to teach Lucien to stand up for himself, to protect himself from the endless jeers that came his way. I wasn't sure how to go about doing this.

While Lucien was away at school I spent many hours resting beneath my Hummingtree. I would lay my fears, my concerns and my frustrations on my rock while I recited my litany of needy questions. The answer was always the same. "He needs you, Ellen. Just be there for him and let him know he is loved."

"Maybe I should take him to a gym and get him some boxing lessons. Or maybe I should go and talk to the parents of these rotten kids who won't stop picking on Lucien."

"No, Ellen," the rock beneath my Hummingtree insisted. "Just be there for him. Nothing else is required of you."

My Hummingtree had never let me down. I needed to keep the faith and know that the advice I received was what I needed to follow. But, I'm a willful woman. I decided that if I couldn't teach Lucien to fight back with his fists, I would teach him to fight back with words.

"Sing this song with me, Lucien," I would say. "Sing loud now! *Sticks and stones may break my bones but words will never hurt me!*"

I taught Lucien how to sing this song. We would sing it together. "Lucien," I said to him in the morning before he set off for school, "remember the song. If any of those kids give you a hard time just sing it loud and clear, okay?"

"Okay, Gram," he said.

I never did hear him singing though. I would hear the teasing taunts of the cruel children and Lucien's silence would break my heart. As he grew older the teasing continued but the bullies no longer gained satisfaction from words alone. They began picking at Lucien. They would form a circle around him and they would push him from one kid to another.

I never saw this happen myself but Lucien told me about it.

"Did you push them back, Lucien?"

"No, Gram."

"You should push them back."

"Okay, Gram."

But, of course, he never did. I told Carol about it.

"I'll talk to his teacher," she said.

Lucien had more than his fair share of troubles in his short life but the day that stands out in my mind is that Tuesday six years ago when Lucien was only ten.

"He's a bit slow in the head," I said to my daughter again that morning.

"Learning difficulties, Mom! He has learning difficulties!"

That afternoon I was out in my front yard watering the plants just as I did every day. School had been let out and children were shouting, laughing and playing on the sidewalk as they passed my house on their way home. This day I did not see Lucien coming.

Soon the sidewalks were silent. All the children had passed by and still there was no sign of Lucien. Panic started in my stomach and by the time it worked its way into my heart my legs had already gone into action. I ran the two blocks up the road to the school.

Lucien was not in the school yard. He was not inside the school. Lucien was nowhere to be found. The teacher tried to calm me down. "He's probably just playing at a friend's house," she said.

I just stared at her. "Playing at a friend's house? Are you Lucien's teacher?"

"Yes, of course."

"Then you must know that Lucien has no friend."

"Come. We will talk to the principal," she replied.

The principal called the police. I went home and I called Carol. "I'm on my way home," she said.

I was fit to be tied. Lucien! Lucien! Where are you, my boy?

I had to do something but what could I do? I left the house and went out into the backyard. I sat on God's good earth beneath my Hummingtree. I prayed to the God in my rock. I prayed harder than I had ever prayed in my life. "Help me, God. Help me find my Lucien."

"Be still, Ellen," the voice whispered. "You will find him in the silence."

Not knowing what else I could do, I did as I was told. I sat beneath my Lilac and listened as the humming in the tree became louder and louder. I was lost in the humming when I began to see Lucien in my mind's eye. The woods! Lucien was in the woods!

I raced to the back gate, left my yard and followed the trail into the woods behind my house. "Lucien! Lucien!" I shouted as I ran.

At long last I heard my boy. "Gram! Help! Over here, Gram!"

I followed the voice through the deep woods until at last I could see him. *Thank you, God, for leading me to my boy.* Aloud I shouted, "I'm coming, Lucien. Gram is here!"

They had tied him to a tree. They had stripped him of his clothes and with clothesline rope they had tied my little Lucien to a tree. In black marker ink they had scrawled the words *PISSY SISSY* across his heaving chest.

"Help me, Gram!" he cried.

As I untied the rope I kept repeating, "It's okay, Lucien. It's okay. Gram is here. I will help you."

I removed my old sweater and wrapped it around his shivering body. "Let's go home, son."

"I don't want to go to school anymore, Gram"

"I know, Lucien. I know."

I made my report to the police. I told Carol everything that had happened.

"I'll talk to his teacher," she said.

"No!" I shouted. "No more! This time I will talk to his teacher. We will find another school for Lucien; one where he fits in. I will not stand by for one more day and watch this boy be victimized by bullies."

Six years ago that is exactly what I did. Today Lucien thrives in his classroom where all the children are a bit slow in the head.

"They have special needs, Mom. Don't say slow in the head."

"All right, special needs! Anyway we are the ones who were slow in the head but thanks to my Hummingtree we are wiser today.

THE FINAL FEAR

It's late. It's dark outside. I force my childish fear of the dark down into my tired feet hoping this will make them tread faster down this unfamiliar dark suburban street. It's a cold October night. My blue woolen jacket is falling down on its job. I'm freezing. I lift my ungloved hand, raise it to my forehead and swipe the cold sweat bubbles into the frosty night air.

I was a fool to fill in for my friend. Yes, I felt sorry for her being sick and a single mom with all those kids to care for but I've been teaching English for enough years to have earned the privilege of avoiding the night school classes. When my friend asked the favour all common sense went on vacation and I allowed pity to make my decision. This is why I have spent this entire evening as a substitute teacher in a college campus way out of my neighbourhood and way out of my comfort zone.

Living and working in the west end of Toronto I get along just fine without a car. Walking takes me everywhere I need to go and it's only a ten minute walk to the college campus where I work the day shift.

Somehow it didn't seem so bad getting to this outreach campus. Yes, it was a fairly lengthy bus ride but then there was only a twenty minute walk from Keele Street where the buses have a regular run. When I got off the bus I found myself in an industrial section. As I walked toward the campus I felt just fine. There were people around several of the buildings I passed. There were cars parked in the factory parking lots. I had never been in this part of town before. I enjoyed the walk to the adult education centre. The autumn sun felt warm on my hatless head.

The three hour class presented no problem. It was uneventful and I enjoyed the adult students' eager willingness to learn. They were so much more dedicated to their purpose than the teenagers I often struggled to teach in the larger main campus on a regular daily basis.

In no time at all the three hour class was over. Now I stand outside the main doors in the dark. I tell myself it is silly to be frightened. After all it is only ten o'clock. I remind myself that I stayed out much later than this when I was a teenager. Oh, but I was never alone at night. Always I was with my girlfriends or maybe on a Friday or a Saturday night I would be with a date who always drove me home to my door.

From the moment I leave the college campus my adrenalin kicks in and my heart starts to quiver. I start walking. I hear the echo of my steps in the dark shadows. I am shocked to discover that once I get out of the range of the campus there are no street lights to brighten the dark fear that is forming in the pit of my stomach.

I watch as the last car passes me. Not one student stopped to ask me if I wanted a ride. How rude is that? But then again, why would they? They don't know me. For all they know I could be Jane the Ripper. Why didn't I ask one of my students to drive me to the bus stop after class? Better yet, why didn't I just say no when my friend asked me to fill in for her?

It's very quiet. I wish I carried a flashlight in my purse. It's a cold, deep dark night. I look up but there is not a star in the sky. The clouds are so black I cannot see their shape. The moon is hiding. I feel alone; too alone. I lift the collar on the back of my blue woolen jacket. Still the frosty tingle of hair raised on the back of my neck sends shivers down my back.

I look around. I see nothing but the occasional factory security light in the far distance. All the factories are closed. There is no one working an evening or a night shift. No, I am the only fool.

I've been walking for maybe five minutes when I remember that the janitor will still be in the school building. Should I turn around and return to the campus and ask him for a drive to the bus stop? My thoughts are scared but alert. They tell me that maybe he has already left the parking lot and driven toward his home in the direction opposite to the one I am walking.

No, I keep walking. I will reach the bus stop in another fifteen minutes, maybe less if I hurry. I quicken my already rapid steps along the cold, hard sidewalk.

From out of nowhere a hand reaches out and grabs me by the collar. There is no one around to hear me screaming. I fall to the cold concrete. I smell tobacco. I barely see the shadow of a large hand; the glint of something shiny. Something very sharp pierces my heart.

***

From this vantage point I can see everything clearly. It's the school janitor. He grabs me by the collar of my blue woolen jacket. He is strong and I watch as he pulls me down to the sidewalk. It's very cold.   And now I can see that he has something hidden in his right hand. With horror I watch as he stabs the shuriken into my heart.

I am floating high above my body now. I no longer feel the physical pain but the emotional fear and disgust stays with me as I watch him remove my slacks. I am lying half naked on the concrete. He opens his trousers and he rapes my defenseless dead body. It is a sad disheartening sight, not something I want to keep

watching. In no time at all I tear my eyes away from the

horror. In the distance I see a white light. I walk

towards it. I step into the light. I feel warm. I feel

protected. Tonight I felt my final fear and now I am at

peace. I am not alone anymore.

I am going home.

■■

IT DOESN'T MATTER

His mother's death brought Mike Patterson Halsten home to Elliot Lake. The funeral had been sparsely attended. Kimberly Patterson had been a woman who preferred spending her time with books rather than wrapping her life with a lot of people. Only one person received her total devotion and that was her son, Miles.

■■■■■■■■■■■■■■■■■■■■■■■■■■■■■■■■■■■■

Driving north on Highway 108 Miles left the town behind him. Memories of his mother kept him company as he drove along the lonely expanse of road. He knew that her life as a single mother has been challenging. He remembered the anger he had felt in his teen years when his mother refused to divulge the identity of his father.

It was a hot day in July, 1989 when Miles impulsively made a sudden turn on to an old logging road. He hadn't driven too far into the bush when he noticed the old trailer. Stopping the car he got out and walked through the knee high weeds to take a closer look. "It's in pretty poor shape," Miles decided, "a real fixer-upper." Walking around the trailer Miles stopped once in a while. Raising himself up on tiptoe, brushing the cobwebs aside, he tried to peek through the dirty windows.

His view was hampered by the neglected glass and by a piece of cardboard taped inside the window. On the cardboard was a phone number that Miles jotted down in his memory. Through dirty windows he couldn't see much but he spotted an older dresser tucked into a corner beside a closet. He could see a table covered with oilcloth. It was no beauty but in spite of this he felt the old trailer had potential. And greater than this fact was a feeling that journeyed

through Miles's body to his heart; an unexplainable

warm feeling that caused him to want to see more.

He strode back to his car, started the engine, and

headed back toward Elliot Lake.   Once back inside his

mother's apartment Miles picked up the phone and

dialed the number. The man who answered the phone

informed Miles that the trailer belonged to an 89 year

old retired Swedish sailor with Alzheimer's who had

been moved to a seniors' residence a few months ago.

Since that time the trailer had been standing vacant.

Without hesitation Miles set up an appointment

with the man who introduced himself as Ronald

Jackson, a lawyer authorized to deal on the owner's

behalf.

The next day was another hot one. Miles

arrived for his appointment and found the agent's car

already parked on the side of the road. Pulling up behind him Miles got out of the car, shook hands with the agent and followed him through the bush to the trailer.

At the trailer door Mr. Jackson offered to stay outside allowing Miles to view the trailer by himself. "There's no surplus of room in there," Ronald laughed patting his rotund belly. "Take your time. I'm in no hurry."

The trailer was basically empty, ready for a buyer to take possession. Miles liked what he saw but more importantly he liked the way he felt. He couldn't explain why he felt so very much at home in a trailer he was seeing for only the second time. No doubt the trailer was far from perfect. There were many things to be fixed but Miles was satisfied.

There and then he stepped outside and made a deal with Mr. Jackson. He wrote out a cheque, signed some papers and the trailer was his to do with as he pleased.

"I'll register these things when I return to town," the lawyer promised. "Consider the trailer yours. I'll be on my way. Here's the key. Good luck!" and he was gone.

Miles walked back into his trailer, took a better look around and discovered that one of the things that needed to be fixed was a dresser that was tucked into a corner beside the closet. Opening one of the drawers in the dresser he saw that the dresser was screwed into the wall. "I can do without this piece of junk," he said to himself. He left the trailer then walked back to his car where he retrieved a screwdriver from his took kit in the trunk.

Back inside the trailer again Miles proceeded to remove the dresser from the wall. The screws were very rusty and it wasn't the easy job he had anticipated. Pulling the small dresser towards him he saw a letter fall from behind it. Curious he picked the letter up. If he hadn't already been on his hands and knees he would have fallen to his knees in shock because written on the sealed envelope was the name Kimberly Patterson, Miles's mother. "How is this possible?" Miles asked the empty space. He noticed the date stamped on the envelope was August 19, 1949. "That's my birth date! How is this possible?"

He slipped the unopened envelope into his pocket to be read later. For now his curiosity drove him to open the two drawers in the dresser. The first drawer seemed filled with bed sheets but when he opened the bottom drawer the other strange thing he found screwed to the back of the drawer was a small, old wooden box that had been glued shut.

Miles unscrewed the box from the back of the dresser drawer. Holding it in his hands he was almost afraid to open it but open it he knew he must. It wasn't easy but with the screwdriver he managed to pry it open without doing too much damage to the box. Miles could not believe what was revealed to him.

With trembling hands he lifted the two photos out of the box. The first tears he had shed since receiving the news of his mother's death tore from his eyes. The smiling young face of his mother looked back at him. "My God," he realized, "this is Mom before I was born. How beautiful she was!"

The second photo showed his mother, Kimberly, standing beside a handsome young man who had his arm around her shoulder. Miles stared long and hard at this picture. Then turning it over he read the scrawl, "Kim Patterson and Bjorn Halsten."

"Dear God," Miles cried realizing that he was meeting his father for the first time.

He held the photos and stared at them for a long time. Then, remembering the envelope, he removed it from his pocket. With trembling fingers he broke the seal and removed a single slip of paper neatly folded in half. Miles wiped the tears from his eyes and read, "Kimberly, my darling, I will love you forever. Forgive me if you can for deceiving you. My wife waits in Helsingborg, Sweden, for this old sailor to return. I know you will be a proud and loving mother to our child. Forgive me please and know I will never forgive myself for not being there for you. Bjorn."

Miles lifted his eyes from the paper then looked around the dusty trailer. The death of his mother had led him to the father he had always wanted and never known. "Thank you, God," he prayed as he returned to his car. He would phone Ronald Jackson for the address and be on his way to meet his father in the seniors' residence. With Alzheimer's would his father remember that he had a child by Kimberly? "It doesn't matter," Miles resolved. "It doesn't matter. The truth has set me free."

FREDDIE'S ATHABASCA

Was it mere happenstance or fate that brought Georgina Berethhamner to Fort McMurray, Alberta, Canada? She never dreamed that they would have the opportunity to leave that depressing refugee camp in Turkey. Her father, Frederick, used to say to Georgina, "Little girl, trust me; one day we will be free from this terrible bondage. Do not be afraid to look beneath what appears to be reality."

Georgina did trust her father but at the age of ten she sometimes found it difficult to look beneath anything or to believe his promises. He would wander the camp and often he would talk to himself. He used to talk to his wife, Gisella, about his dream of living freely in a home on the Athabasca River. Georgina's mother had faith in her husband. While most people called him Frederick, his wife Gisella, called him her Freddie.

Gisella would also sometimes wander the camp. To her friends she would talk about her Freddie's Athabasca. And when she talked her eyes would brighten a cloudy day. Georgina thought her mother was beautiful. Her father, Freddie, thought so too. He would call Gisella his daisy in a weed patch.

For a long time Georgina lived from day to depressing day with her parents in the refugee camp in Turkey. On her twelfth birthday the blue sky turned black and crashed down upon her. Gisella died. "Why did mama die, papa?" she begged.

"She was too beautiful to live in such an ugly place," Freddie responded. "She didn't belong here, child."

Then with a determination that frightened Georgina he shouted for all in the camp to hear, "And neither do you! Neither do you belong here, my little one."

Georgina didn't like it when her father cried. It frightened her. It seemed that everything frightened her and so she cried along with him.

"Don't cry, Georgina," her father soothed. "One day soon we will leave this cesspool and travel to Canada. Do not accept what you see on the surface of life. Look beneath. Trust me, child."

She did. And one day, to her amazement, she and her father were passengers in an airliner bound for Fort McMurray, Alberta.

They lived in a small house not far from the Athabasca River. Georgina was elated to be living in Freddie's Athabasca but she missed her mother,

Gisella, more than she could bear. She learned from her father that the Athabasca River, a tributary of the Mackenzie, was 764 miles long and that it ran from a small lake at the base of Mount Brown in the Rocky Mountains called Committee's Punchbowl.

She thought the lake had a very strange name indeed but not nearly as strange as the name the neighbourhood children gave to her. Birthhammer, they called her. She was already scared to be in this big, strange, new country and in their shouts Georgina detected a meanness that frightened her even more. She wanted to tell them that her name was not Birthhammer. She was Georgina Berethhamner and she had a right to be living freely in Freddie's Athabasca. She wanted to set the neighbourhood children straight but she couldn't. She spoke no English.

Freddie spoke a little English, enough to get by, at his new job in Canada. He worked on the large tar sand deposits found southwest of Lake Athabasca not too far from Fort McMurray or as he and Georgina learned to call their new home, Fort Mac.

Compared to the refugee camp in Turkey, Fort Mac was paradise. Georgina absorbed the beauty of the mountains, ponds and lakes. Yes, she missed Gisella, her mother, but in this strange new land she felt a peace and a safety that she had never felt before. She thought Freddie's Athabasca was a lovely place but she knew she could never experience true happiness in her new home until she learned to speak its native tongue; English.

Frederick enrolled his daughter in the local elementary school and set off to work where he helped to extract the oil from the sand. He explained to

106

Georgina the amazing modern technology that made it possible for men to extract oil from beneath the sand.

"Do you see, daughter?" he would ask. "Do you see what I mean when I say it is essential that we look beneath that which appears to be reality? Why, to look at the sand one would never dream there would be precious oil beneath. And you must always remember that when we looked beneath our dreary existence in the refugee camp we found the beauty of my Athabasca."

Georgina dreaded having to go to school. It was bad enough that the other children made fun of her poor language skills but that was made worse by their taunts of *Brainless Birthhammer*! It took several months but Georgina did find herself surprised by her own ability to learn a new language. But she found English very difficult to learn.

"How can one word be spelled in so many different ways and mean different things?" she asked her father. "How can one know whether to write the word to, too or two in a sentence?

Freddie, though he spoke English reasonably well, was not well-versed in its spelling or grammatical aspects. Not liking to admit his ignorance he would encourage his daughter to make good use of the dictionary he had bought for her. Look the words up, Georgina; learn their meanings.

And so she did. By Georgina's fourteenth birthday she was, like her father, reasonably fluent in English. And by the time she was fourteen she was ready to enroll in the local high school. Freddie did his best to give guidance and advice to his daughter but there were things in a girl's life that only a mother could provide. And these were the things Georgina missed.

When she remembered Gisella she remembered her beauty, her faith and her loyalty. This was the example set by her mother that Georgina did her best to follow.

A naturally pretty girl, she decided to look beneath those things that were lacking in her life and in doing so she discovered strengths and abilities within herself that she didn't know existed. She worked hard. Through study and determination she learned to love the English language. She surprised herself by winning a provincial writing competition. Of all the high school entries in Alberta, Georgina's story took the prize. She was beginning to believe that in Freddie's Athabasca anything was possible.

"I'm very proud of you, daughter; very proud," Freddie told her. "One day you will write books and you will be famous and people all over the world will know your name."

"Oh, papa, that would be wonderful but I would be happy if just the kids in this neighbourhood would get my name straight. Still they call me Berthhammer. Will they never stop?"

"It doesn't matter, Georgina. Maybe they will never stop but do you need to care? You know who you are. You are the lovely, creative daughter of the beautiful Gisella."

And time passed as it has a way of doing even in Fort McMurray, Alberta. Life for Georgina was good in her Freddie's Athabasca. She graduated high school and went on to gain her higher education at the University of Alberta. She became a scientist and held an important position in the modern technological world in Fort McMurray.

It was a sad day when her father passed away. By then Georgina was happily married and mother to a smart little Canadian boy who would sometimes complain to his mother when things didn't go his way. "Look beneath, my son," she would encourage. "Go beneath what you think is the reality. You will be surprised what you can discover about yourself."

And one day Georgina retired. She became a grandmother. Her world in Freddie's Athabasca was filled with a satisfying sense of accomplishment. Yet something was missing. No matter her age she still sometimes felt the pangs of loneliness that she had experienced as an immigrant child. She still remembered the cruel taunts of the children, *"Brainless Birthhammer!"*

She thought of her father. Look beneath, she knew he would advise. And so she did. She decided she would write her memoirs. I will call it Freddie's Athabasca, she decided.

Picking up a pen she opened her journal and wrote. *I have been called Brainless Berthhammer. I have been called many things I would rather not remember. But today I make my stand and I say to all who will listen; my name is Georgina Berethhamner. I am the daughter of Gisella and Frederick. My mother had faith and my father had determination. These are the things that brought me to Freddie's Athabasca. Look beneath the surface and you will discover I am more than I ever dreamed I could be.*

I NEED YOU TO REMEMBER ME

"You think I don't hear the gossip!" I exclaim in indignation. "What are you trying to insinuate? Just because I'm a little forgetful doesn't mean anything."

"I'm not insinuating anything, Mom. David and I were just talking about an ad we saw in the paper this morning."

"Ad, schmad! I see the way you two look at each other. Guess I know what's going on! I didn't just fall off the turnip truck!"

"You've got it all wrong, Mom," David intercepts. "When we saw the Happy Haven ad Francine and I just thought this would be a good day to take a drive and have a look at the place. Did you know the retirement residence overlooks the inlet? Beautiful view and the grounds are ideal for a picnic by the lake."

"It will do us all some good to get out of the city and enjoy some fresh air," Francine agrees.

"Lots of good places along the lakeshore for a picnic if that's what you're looking for," I say. "I know what you're up to! You want to be rid of me! You want to put me into a home!" I can feel my hope for freedom falling. It lands like sediment at the bottom of my stomach. "I have a stomach ache!" I declare. "Can't go anywhere today!"

I pull the belt snug on my blue chenille robe and leaving the kitchen I walk through the living-room on my way to my bedroom. I hear my daughter shout, "It's time to get dressed, Mom. We'll take a nice drive in the car today."

"Have a nice time, dear," I shout back just before closing my door.

My stomach doesn't feel quite so heavy once I'm back in my room. I sit on the bed and, arms by my side, I run my hands back and forth on the silky softness of the bedspread. I know it was a gift from somebody. Now who was that? It wasn't all that long ago. Oh, well, it's not important who it came from. It's not as though I'm planning to give it back.

I get up from my bed and walk over to my dressing table. Opening the middle drawer I rummage for my underwear. It's time to get dressed. I feel like going for a walk. I see my shoes on the floor over by the armchair; the comfortable ones. I'll wear them today. Now what am I looking for? I keep rummaging around in the drawer but I can't find it, whatever it is.

Now what was I going to do? Oh, that's right; I will go for a walk. I cross my room, sit in the armchair and ease my feet into the sensible soft-soled shoes.

I leave my bedroom and cross the living-room to the front door. In the building's hallway I have to stop and think for a minute. Should I go left or right for the elevator? Silly old fool, I chide myself. I'd forget my own head if it wasn't attached to my neck. Of course the elevator is to my right.

I start walking along the hall when I hear some woman calling me.

"Mom, what are you doing?"

Nosy neighbor! Where does she get off calling me Mom? I'm going to tell Francine about this one. I decide to ignore her. I'm just about at the elevator when the woman grabs my arm.

"Hey, lady," I shout. "What's the big idea?"

"Mom, what are you doing?"

"Look lady, I don't know what your problem is but I'm not your mother. Let go of my arm."

"You're not dressed, Mom. You can't go out in your robe!" the woman insists.

I lower my eyes and see that I'm still wearing my blue chenille robe. For heaven's sakes, I forgot to get dressed.

"I'm going home to get dressed now," I tell the lady.

"Let me help you, dear," she says.

"I'm not helpless, you know!" But I decide to let her take my arm and guide me back to my apartment. I'm not really sure if I should turn left or right. "I live in apartment 634."

"I'll take you home, Mom" she says.

"My name is Esther. Just because I'm old enough to be your mother doesn't give you the right to call me Mom. Only Francine can call me that. Well, David too if he wants but I'm not really his Mom."

The lady starts to cry. What's her problem? I'm surprised she opens the door of my apartment and walks right in; doesn't even knock on the door. The nerve of some people's kids!

David is there in the living-room. "You need to get dressed, Mom," he says.

"I know that, David."

"We don't like you wandering off on your own like that."

"I wasn't wandering, David. I was going for a walk. Where is Francine?"

"I'm here, Mom," the stranger says.

"David, you better deal with this woman. I think she's got a few loose screws, if you know what I mean."

I watch as the eyes of this woman and David exchange some sort of silent message. "You two know each other?" I ask. "What are you up to, David?"

I don't hang around to hear his answer.

Back in my room I decide to get dressed. I remove my robe; lay it across the foot of my bed. My pretty yellow nightgown is very comfortable. I've owned it forever. I remember when my mother gave it to me on my 50th birthday. I feel heaviness in my chest as I remember her funeral. It was just a few weeks after my fiftieth. This pretty yellow nightgown means the world to me.

I cross the room and sit in my armchair. Thoughts of Mom and Dad warm my heart. I remember how much my mother loved little Francine. The day she was born my dad started a trust fund for his grand-daughter. That trust fund put Francine through university. I remember it all so clearly. My memory is good! What is it with Francine and David? They tell me I'm forgetful! What do they know? I remember everything. I even remember the names of my primary school teachers. I enjoy this remembering.

I guess I nodded off a little because the next thing I know Francine is there shaking my arm to wake me up. She reminds me of someone else though I can't remember who. "What do you want, Francine?"

"I want you to get dressed, Mom. I've come to help you. Which dress will you wear today?"

"I don't think I'll bother getting dressed today, Francine. I'm very comfortable in my yellow gown. I remember when my mother gave this to me. Did you know it was on my 50th birthday?"

"Yes, Mom, I know. I've heard the story before. Your birthday is not far off. What do you want for your 86th ?"

"86th ? You'd never know this nightgown was that old, would you now?" I ask wondering how on earth I got to be eighty-six years old.

"What about this soft green dress? You always liked wearing this one, didn't you?"

"It's okay. Why do I need to get dressed?"

"Didn't you say you wanted to go for a walk?"

"That's right," I remember. "It's a nice day. I want to go for a walk."

"David and I are going to take you for a nice drive this morning, Mom."

"No drive! I told you I want to go for a walk!"

"We are going to drive along the lakeshore to a nice park where we can all enjoy a lovely walk, okay?"

"Bossy pants! Always have to have things your way! You always were a stubborn child, Francine!"

"Please, Mom. You look so pretty in this dress. It brings out the green in your eyes."

"It does?" Her compliment lifts my spirits. "Yes, a nice walk in a park by the lake; that's just what I want to do."

She helps me into the dress, and then plays with my hair saying, "Okay, you're ready to go."

"Go? Where am I going, Francine? And where's my handbag? I don't want to go out without my handbag."

She gives me one of those long drawn-out God-in-Heaven-help-me sighs and gives me my handbag which I carry over my arm. Taking my other arm she walks with me out of the apartment, along the hallway to the elevator.

Outside the building we reach the roadside where I see David sitting behind the wheel of his car. "Are you going to work now, David?" Not waiting for an answer I tell him, "Francine and I are going for a walk in the park now."

"Yes, I know," he says. "I'm going to drive you both to the park. Get in the car, Mom."

"Oh, okay. That's very nice of you, David."

Francine opens the car door wide. "You get into the back seat with me."

"You don't need to be so bossy, Francine!"

To David I say, "Don't drive too fast. Remember! I don't like driving fast!"

I see the lovely blue water of Lake Ontario as we drive along the lakeshore. We pass the boardwalk and I remember when I walked there with my boyfriend long ago. I remember the day I married my boyfriend. I walked with him and pushed Francine in her pram along that boardwalk.

"Driver, stop the car!" I shout.

The car keeps moving. "Francine, tell the driver to stop this taxi at once!"

"Mom," Francine says, "we don't want to stop. We are going to the park for a nice walk, remember?"

"Don't want to go to a park. I want to walk on the boardwalk! If you won't make the driver stop, I'll stop him myself." I swing my handbag and whack him a good one on the back of his head.

"Ow!" the driver cries.

"Mom, stop it!" Francine yells as she yanks the handbag out of my hands.

"Give me back my purse!"

"I will, Mom, when we get to the park."

Soon the taxi pulls off the road. I see we are on a very long driveway and soon I can see a very large house; so big I think it must be a hotel. The driver keeps going past the hotel and carries on down the road until he comes to a park. I can see the water now. The lake is very calm. This is a very nice place to go for a walk.

The driver stops the car and opens the back door to assist me as I get out. I'm surprised to see the driver is David. "Thank you, David. I didn't know you were going to walk with us today. This is very pleasant."

There is a lovely path along the water's edge. I slip my arm through Francine's and together we begin our walk. David walks on my other side. I don't take his arm because I need to carry my handbag.

"What's the name of that big hotel we passed?"

"I'm not sure," David responds.

"I don't know, Mom," Francine answers.

"Let's walk up that way," David suggests. "We can go inside for a nice cup of tea. Would you like that, Mom?"

I would and I tell him so.

As we draw closer to the hotel I can see the sign over the main door. It says *Happy Haven*.

I'm on to them. "You tricked me! You lied to me!"

"No, Mom," David says. "Why all the fuss? We're just going in for a cup of tea. Didn't you say you wanted a cup of tea?"

"Yes, I did, didn't I?"

"It's okay, Mom," Francine says. "This is a nice place."

"How nice, Francine? I'm just wearing my old walking shoes."

"Mom, you are so pretty in your green dress. No one is going to notice your shoes."

"Well, if you're sure."

"I'm sure," she smiles.

Inside the hotel I take a good look around. There are round tables with armchairs and there are a couple of sofas. I even see some lawn chairs through the glass doors that lead out to a deck. It is a nice place. "But Francine, how come all the hotel guests are so old? I feel like I'm in a mausoleum!"

We sit at a table. We wait for a waitress. We wait a long time. I look around at all the bald heads and the gaping mouths on the sleeping old women. What kind of a hotel is this?

The waitress arrives but I notice she looks more like a nurse than a waitress. "What is going on here?"

I see David whisper something to the hospital waitress and she goes away.

Again we wait. "Service is slow," I say.

The sun's rays through the glass deck doors feel good but make me sleepy.

Then "Wake up, Mom," I hear Francine yelling.

I open my eyes to see a young woman wearing light blue scrubs. She places the mug on the table in front of me. "Here's a nice cup of tea for you, Esther."

"Thank you." Then, I ask Francine and David, "Aren't you having tea?"

"No, Mom," she says. "You drink your tea and then we'll do a wander around the hotel. Would you like that?"

"No, I want to walk outside by the water."

"We'll do that after we check out the hotel, Mom," David says.

"Bossy pants! Always have to do things your way!"

I finish drinking my tea. We leave the dining room and I walk around the hotel with them.

"Nice place, eh, Mom?"

The next thing I know David opens a door and leads me into one of the hotel rooms. I see a bed by the window. I see an armchair not much different from the one I have at home in my bedroom. It's even the same colour. I see a bookshelf and as I run my finger along the backs of the books I think it's odd that the shelf holds some of the very books I own. Then I notice a couple of photos. How very odd! I see a photo of a bride and groom. When I look closely I see that the bride is me. I see another photo of Francine and David atop a dresser. This is very strange. I'm confused. I pinch my arm to see if I'm awake.

I decide to open one of the drawers in the dresser. In the top drawer I see my pretty yellow nightgown; the very one my mother gave to me on my 50th birthday.

I turn around to look at Francine and David. I see the waitress wearing the medical scrubs is also there in the room with them. "What's going on, Francine? Where are we?"

"Why, we are in your room, Mom," David replies.

"In my room?"

I move to the window. Looking through the windowpane I see the lovely park. I see the blue water and the path that runs along beside the lake.

"I want to go for a walk."

"Sure, Mom," Francine says. I see David look at the waitress. She smiles and nods.

"Who are you?" I ask her.

"I'm Susan," she says.

"Oh," I say. I don't remember her but I don't need to let them know I've forgotten something again. "Are you coming for a walk with us?"

"Sure," she says.

The walk by the lake is pleasurable.   I'm feeling a little tired.

"Ready to go back to your room, Mom?" Francine asks.

"Yes, I think so. Maybe I'll take a little nap."

"Good idea," David says.

Back in my room I sit on the edge of my bed. I look at Francine, David and Susan. "Why are you all hanging about in my room? Don't you have anything better to do?"

"Mom, do you have everything you need? Is there anything you would like me to bring when we come to visit you?"

"Come to visit me? Francine, what on earth are you talking about?"

"Nothing, Mom. You just rest. We'll see you soon."

I recline on my bed. I move my hands back and forth on the familiar silky softness of my bedspread. I allow my gaze to travel to the photos on my dresser; the books on my shelf. Everything looks the same yet somehow it all seems different. I move my gaze to the window. Getting up from my bed I walk to the window and looking out I see the blue water. I don't remember having a lake outside my bedroom window. How on earth could I forget something like that?

"Francine, there's a lake outside my window."

"Yes, Mom," she says. "Why not come back to bed and have a little nap?"

"Yes, I think I'll do that."

I remember when I'm a little girl and my mother tells me it's nap time. I look around for my mother but she's not in the room. I see a tall man. I see a woman who is familiar. Her name is on the tip of my tongue but I can't recall it. There's another person there and by the way she's dressed she should be in a hospital; not here in my room. Who are these people?

"We're leaving now," the familiar one says. "Is there anything you need?"

I'm very sleepy; too tired to wait for Mommy to come tuck me in. To the strange people I don't know what to say. Do I need anything? I'm having some difficulty remembering who I am. I can't think of anything I need. To satisfy them and to get them out of my room I say, "Sometimes I forget so I need you to remember me."

They close my door behind them. I was beginning to think they would never leave. I roll over onto my side and welcome sleep.

DESTINY

They are at it again. Mom's high screech competes with Dad's harsh deep rumble, a hellish cacophony. I'm wearing my headphones but even with Kelly Clarkson's lyrics at the highest volume I can't drown out the selfish sound of their shared misery.

Kelly sings, *"What doesn't kill you makes you stronger, stronger. Just me, myself and I. What doesn't kill you makes you stronger, Stand a little taller. Doesn't mean I'm lonely when I'm alone."*

Fallout from my parents' marriage hasn't killed me, at least not yet. Has it made me stronger? That I'm ready to find out. I've made my plan and soon I will celebrate my

136

long-awaited independence. I've had enough of living in this zoo. I want my freedom now.

Last month I read in Teen Vogue Magazine that Kelly Clarkson lives somewhere outside of Fort Worth, Texas but Texas is not where I'm heading. I'm preparing myself to get to Nashville, Tennessee. Somehow I'll find a way to get myself up onto the stage of the Grand Old Opry.

I'm Kelly's number one fan and lots of people have told me my voice is every bit as good as hers. Tennessee is a long way from my small nowhere northern town but I've been saving for nearly five years since I was eleven. I have more than enough money to pay my bus fare. I've saved enough to cover my living expenses for at least a month. Will that be enough time for me to get a foot in the show business door? I can only hope so. When my parents named me Destiny it was probably the last time they did anything positive. Everything between them has been going downhill since the day I was born sixteen years ago.

I'm not your average runaway. I have travel plans. If Gil Grand can do it, so can I. I read about Gil Grand in another of my teen magazines. In 1998 when I was just two years old he left his home town of Sudbury and travelled to Nashville where he signed to a major U.S. record deal with Sony Music Nashville's Monument Records. In no time at all he received three CCMA nominations for male vocalist of the year, album of the year and something called Wrangler Rising Star which I am not sure what that means but still Gil's success tells me I can succeed. It is possible.

Just like Gil I can go on tour with the big names; maybe not the Dixie Chicks the way he did, but maybe, if my deepest dream could be realized, I could sing with Kelly Clarkson.

I removed my headset and put it on my dresser before pulling my desk chair over to my clothes closet. Being an only child I don't have to share anything with anybody. I hear Mom's sobbing now. She does a lot of crying once she's grown tired of yelling and screaming. This is her usual routine. For the moment Dad is silent. This too is typical. I stand up on the chair and hope I can reach the old brown suitcase that sits on the closet's top shelf. I grab hold of the handle, give it a good yank. I'm just about to step down from the chair when their ruckus starts again.

"What did you do with the money?" Dad screams. "Answer me, damn it! What did you do with the money I gave you?"

I carry the suitcase over to my bed, undo the zipper and open it. I rustle through my dresser drawers and it doesn't take me long to pack my favourite jeans, a few tops, some underwear and my make-up bag. I will travel light.

"Maybe you think I spent the afternoon at the spa?" Mom shouts. "I should be so lucky! What do you think I did with the money? I paid the gas bill and I bought some groceries,"

I don't want to hear Dad's response so I put my headset back on. *Thanks to you I got a new thing started. Thanks to you I'm not the broken-hearted. Thanks to you I'm finally thinking about me ...."* I sing along with Kelly.

Atop my clothes I place a couple pairs of shoes in a plastic bag, my favourite CD's, my camera and my cell phone.

I haven't packed much; just the one suitcase. There are still tons of clothes and shoes in my bedroom closet. My parents are so absorbed in their familiar futility that they never know when I'm here anyway. I figure I can be a long way from home before they even know I'm gone. I take off the headset, place it on top of everything then zip up my suitcase. I stand it by my bedroom window.

Should I leave a note? Yes, maybe I will. I sure don't want the police out after me. I sit down at my desk, pick up a pen and start to write. *"Dear Mom and Dad, it's time for me to venture out on my own. Don't worry about me. I'll write when I get where I'm going. Love,*

Destiny." With a piece of scotch tape I fasten my note onto the dresser mirror.

"You don't give me enough money to run the house properly!" Mom shouts as I lift the window high enough for me to climb through onto the ground outside.

"Yeah, yeah, you're breaking my heart!" Dad screams back.

Am I? Am I breaking any hearts, I wonder, as I push my suitcase through the window and then climb through behind it. Standing outside the house I reach up and lower my bedroom window. I no longer hear the angry voices. Suitcase in hand I make my way toward the bus station where I will board a bus bound for Sudbury. From Sudbury I'll follow Gil Grand's footsteps toward Nashville country music fame and fortune. One day my voice will make me famous. My name is Destiny and I'm

not your average runaway. Maybe once I have a

number one hit on the radio my parents will

finally stop fighting long enough to listen to me.

WHILE YOU WERE SLEEPING

In the year 1208 life was indeed short. By the time a boy was twelve he was considered old enough to swear an oath of allegiance to the king, while a girl was often married before she entered her teen years. Life was difficult and strenuous and most peasants had spent their energies by the time they were in their thirties or forties. Without exception, a man was considered old by the time he reached the age of thirty-five. Walter Leofrick was one of a few in his village to achieve this status and being a poor peasant it was an achievement well-earned.

Since the recent death of his wife, Lucinda, in the cold, wet spring of the year. Walter lived alone in his one room house in the village of Gainsthorpe in the larger County of Lincolnshire, England.

As a rule he would spend his early morning hours tending his garden. Since everything he planted prospered, Walter was said to possess a green thumb. For many years he had served the Lord of the Manor by building and maintaining the roads and fences on the land but in these, his later years, he had grown too tired and dismayed. He had lost all desire to go to work each day as he had faithfully done prior to Lucinda's death.

Unlike most of his peasant neighbours who were farmers, Walter's only farming activity was maintaining his small garden where he now spent much time. It was from here that he garnered the food to keep body and soul together. His country garden contained potatoes, onions, carrots, green runner beans and tomatoes to nourish his rotund tummy as well as roses, chrysanthemums, dahlias. From the surrounding fields came the wild black-eyed Susans, white daisies and the purple blush of heather to provide sustenance for his soul.

Walter took no credit for the creation of this garden. The original perennial plantings were accomplished by Lucinda whose love of nature created what was to become a feast for the eye as well as the stomach.

Twenty years earlier he had built with sticks and straw the house to which he carried his young bride, Lucinda, over the threshold. Its one room contained the hearth which also served as an oven where the young Lucinda baked the bread. There was no chimney in the thatched roof and the house was often very dark and smoky. This accepted condition made the country garden all the more a desirable and glorious place to be. In years past, until she became ill, Lucinda tended the garden. Under her care the garden thrived. She planted, weeded and watered.

All these duties she did and, indeed, she took pride in her gardening. These tasks she completed without complaint. In addition she cleaned the house and cooked their meals. By nature an artistic woman, from her garden she gathered the vegetables with which she made dyes to colour their clothes red, blue or green. She sewed by talented hand making her long skirts and the tunics worn by her husband. Neither Walter nor Lucinda owned a lot of clothing but that which they did possess was of the highest quality and Lucinda, being a very clean woman; clean of body, mind and spirit, kept the clothes spotless unlike many of her neighbours who were more inclined to be slothful and, in many cases, unkempt and careless in their dress. She carried out all these household chores without complaint.

Lucinda's only regret, one shared by Walter, was that no child had been born of their marriage. In spite of this disappointment, or perhaps even because of it, Lucinda was always, without exception, a loving and dutiful wife. Each day she worked hard while Walter made his way down the rutted road each morning to commence working on the property of the Lord of the Manor.

The Manor House far outshone that of Walter and Lucinda containing as it did two rooms; one, the home of the hearth in the main living room, the other being the kitchen containing a large stone oven. Apart from an orange tabby who had been Lucinda's delightful pet, Walter owned no animals but those of his master were housed in a separate building; a wooden barn. The Lord of the Manor also had another separate building which was used to store the crops which were grown on the land all around the house.

Walter never envied the wealth of his master. Throughout his life with the lovely Lucinda he was a happy man until that dire, dreadful day when her sickness struck with a vengeance.

The bloody flux stole Lucinda away. For too long she suffered with dysentery, growing weaker by the day, until the Good Lord arrived at the small cottage, held her hand and led her to her eternal home. Three years younger than her husband, she had been a clever and capable child bride of twelve years. This day she died at the old age of thirty-two.

Devastated, Walter became a shadow of his former self.

It was Walter's good fortune that the Lord of the Manor was a kindly man with a compassionate heart. He recognized Walter's inability to deal well with the loss of his wife. He acknowledged that maybe not too much need be expected of a man of Walter's longevity. He had been a strong and willing worker for twenty years; much longer than most of the peasants who reported daily to fulfill their jobs maintaining the animals in the barns, the grains in the fields and the ruts in the narrow, winding dirt roads. His long duration of service had earned him the respect and admiration of his employer. A quiet, lonely man, Walter was no longer required to work for the Lord of the Manor. He was allowed the privilege of retirement and with gratitude was permitted to remain in the cottage he had built and maintained over the years.

Since his wife's passing, Walter no longer slept well throughout the long, lonely nights. He would lie awake yearning for the warm, loving caress of his lovely Lucinda. Sometimes in his desperate wanting he would forget, if only for a moment, that she no longer shared his bed and he would reach out as he had always done to wrap his arms around her small, soft body.

When he did manage to sleep, it would be a fitful one filled with dreams of vast oceans devoid of water; endless skies empty of clouds or an unwelcoming, brown earth without inhabitants where he would walk for hours seeking a tender touch, an assuring voice or a sympathetic smile. Sometimes in his dream he would catch a fleeting glance of what he believed was a compassionate companion but when he extended his arm and reached out his hand to hold onto something of warm welcome it would disappear behind a rock or in a tree's bouquet of leaves or beneath the deep green grass which covered the burial spot of his beloved Lucinda.

Loneliness filled the days of Walter Leofrick. His nights belonged to a relentless restless search for a peace that could never be found.

Never, that is, until this past night; the night of the visitation.

Walter had learned of the legend of the succubus long ago. In his boyhood he had strained his ears to listen to the men in the village who had whispered of the fatal, female demon who took the form of a human woman in order to seduce men. He knew that this supernatural being visited in dreams when a man was most vulnerable and unable to fend off her sensual and, indeed, sexual advances.

But Walter never dreamed that a succubus would dare to enter the marriage bed he had shared with the lovely Lucinda for twenty years. Never, that is, until this past night when, to his deep despair, the dirty deed was done.

It was as though he were paralyzed; locked in his prisoner bed, a victim, of the demonic temptress.

Unable to offer resistance she had her way with him. As if this was not bad enough, Walter, to his shame, enjoyed the experience.

As a rule Walter would spend his early morning hours tending his garden but not this morning. When he awakened and dragged his used, degraded body from his bed he knew, without doubt, what needed to be done.

Dressed in his best tights and tunic belted at the waist, he covered himself in the blue hooded cape that his dear Lucinda had sewn for him only three years ago. He set off on his long journey to Brauncewell, a town in Lincolnshire he had never before visited though he had heard tales repeated of the large windmill that existed there; a windmill that overshadowed the chapel in which the monks toiled and prayed.

Walter did not give any consideration to visiting the small chapel existent in Gainsthorpe. No, indeed. He knew that to combat the Succubus he needed the wisdom and sound advice of one much wiser than the local minister whose lips, he knew, would not be closed once they tasted the delight of gossiping with Walter's own neighbours about the sordid, sexual, sinful events taking place in the deep dark of night under the thatched roof of Walter Leofrick.

For two days Walter walked. At night he lay in the fields but he dared not sleep lest the Succubus make another visitation. Instead he stared at the starry sky and thought only of his lost Lucinda.

It was late in the day when he reached the Town of Brauncewell. Stopping neither to eat nor drink he made straightaway for the chapel. Upon entering its coolness he genuflected before the massive wooden cross that carried the carved body of the crucified

Christ hanging on the wall above a myriad of candles which had been lit by sojourners praying for peace.

Exhausted mentally, physically and spiritually, Walter was startled when he heard the soft masculine voice behind him.

"How may I help you, my son?"

Walter turned to face the young priest. He looked but found no threat in the brown eyes that searched his own. The monk repeated, "How may I help you, my son?"

"I need to confess. I need the help that only God can give, Father."

"Come with me," the priest said and he led Walter to the small confessional.

Seated on the hard, wooden stool Walter faced forward while he listened to the young monk's voice on the other side of the booth's partition. For the first time since Lucinda's death, he felt free to cry and sob, indeed, he did.

In his wisdom the priest said nothing, allowing Walter to release his pain through his tears. In a few moments the crying ceased. The two men shared silence that hung heavy in the still air. Then at last the silence was broken.

"Forgive me, Father, for I have sinned. It has been many months since my last confession."

From the other side of the screen Walter heard, "Go ahead, son. Speak freely. Our God is a loving God."

"Father, I am sure I have committed many sins but I have made this long journey from Gainsthorpe to see you because I have been victimized by a Succubus. Two nights ago this demon entered my bed while I slept. She forced herself upon me and I was, indeed, unfaithful to my beautiful Lucinda who died not long ago. Father, she raped me. I have done the unforgivable and now I dare not sleep ever again."

"In God's eyes nothing is unforgivable, my son. Let God hear your Act of Contrition"

Again Walter was overwhelmed by sadness but through his tears he prayed, "Oh my God, I am heartily sorry for having offended Thee. I fear the fires of Hell and, please dear God; I need your help to keep the demon Succubus away from me so that I may sleep without fear of offending Thee. With your help I firmly resolve to go forth and sin no more but, Lord God, I am at your mercy. I don't know how to keep the demon out of my sleeping bed." He sobbed.

"Walter," the monk said, "your penance is to pray twelve Our Father's and seven Hail Mary's."

"Yes, Father," I will do as you say but is there nothing more I can do to ensure that the Succubus does not return to have her way with me?"

For a few minutes the priest was silent and thoughtful. When he spoke he surprised Walter by asking him a question. "Do you know how to work with wood, Walter? Have you ever done any wood carving?"

"Not really, Father," Walter replied. But then he remembered. "A long time ago when I was but a boy I did make a whistle. I hollowed out a small branch and carved out the little holes. I did actually find I was able to play some tunes, Father, though not very well, I confess."

"Here is what I want you to do, Walter. I want you to carve a wind chime, one with seven pieces hanging which will make a small tune when disturbed

158

by wind or by spirit? Is this something you think you can accomplish?"

"Yes, Father, I am sure I can accomplish this task."

"Good, Walter! And once you have created this wind chime I want you to hang it over the door of your house. In this way when the Succubus spirit enters your home she will cause the chimes to sound and this way awaken you from sleep. A succubus cannot enter the body of one who is awake, my son. Do you understand?"

"Yes, Father, I do understand. Thank you. I will return home and I vow I will not sleep again until I have made the wind chime and have it hung over the door of my home."

"And now, my son, go forth and sin no more."

"Thank you, Father."

Walter left the chapel and once out on the road he wasted no time in beginning his tasks. As he walked he repeated the Our Father's a dozen times and seven times he recited aloud the Hail Mary's. Feeling lighter somehow he allowed his eyes to wander as he travelled. When he spotted the Willow tree he became almost enthusiastic.

He retained a boyhood memory that the best whistles were made from either the Willow or the Maple tree. He left the road and sauntered over to the Willow tree. Good fortune was on his side as it was the spring of the year. Walter knew that to remove the bark from a Willow twig was something that could be done only in the spring when there was more sap rising up the tree making the bark more easily removable.

Walter chose a Willow branch that was approximately one inch in diameter. He knew that he would need to cut the branch in order to make the seven chimes that would hang down. Thinking each chime would need to be at least seven inches in length he chose a branch that was more than fifty inches long.

As he walked he retrieved his knife from the pocket of his tunic and began cutting through the bark, circling the branch all the way around. Once this was done he broke another small branch from a tree and with it he bruised his willow stick by tapping on it to loosen the bark. He was then able to slip the bark off after a while. He did this while he walked toward home, taking care to ensure that he didn't split the bark. He didn't want to have to start all over again.

Walter then cut a few notches into the wood; seven notches to be exact equally spaced along the length of the willow branch. He then shaved off thin slivers from the wood to form airways. Then with his knife he cut the branch into seven separate pieces. Once he reached home he would tie these seven pieces with string to a block of wood and all of this together would be his wind chime; one that he would hang over the door of his house to keep the Succubus at bay.

The making of the seven pieces was a tedious task but one that Walter found he was actually enjoying. For the first time since the death of Lucinda he was able to clear his mind and focus on the task at hand. He felt awake. Not just the sluggish awake due to lack of sleep but something greater than this. He felt not simply awake. Rather, Walter felt an awakening; a raising of his consciousness; a greater connection to spirit, that of Lucinda's and, indeed, to that of God himself.

Soon the Village of Gainsthorpe came into view. When Walter drew near to his home he held tight to the seven pieces laying them aside only long enough to gather the block of wood and the string with which he fashioned the wind chime. Fastening it over his door frame he felt the beginning of a smile; the first in a long time to transform his face and his heart.

In his mind's eye he pictured the beautiful Lucinda. He watched as she bent her slim neck and raised her loving blue eyes upward. Then, with gentleness, she breathed on the wind chime creating just enough of a breeze to make the chimes sing. In some unfathomable way Walter's hearing of the song was a vindication. He no longer felt violated by the Succubus. The violation was replaced by forgiveness and love.

Once a shadow of his former self, Walter now lived in the moment; alive, awake and at peace. He found he was able to commune with Lucinda in such a way that she was teaching him to be conscious of his awakening; in touch with nature of which he was, indeed, a part.

Walter worked in his garden each morning. The slightest breeze would make the wind chimes sing reminding him that evil could enter a body only when that body was asleep. And with the aid of Lucinda who was willing to share her knowledge with him, Walter came to understand that a man could be, indeed, asleep even as he carried on his daily duties seemingly alert and with eyes open. But thanks to the Succubus and Lucinda's love, he learned the true meaning of wakefulness.

That night and for every night that followed until he, at last, was permitted to make the journey that reunited him with Lucinda forever, Walter remained ever awake and his sleep was sound.

THE SUPPORT WORKER

My name is Peter and I'm innocent. I didn't do it, I tell you. For verification purposes I guess you need my last name. My full name is Peter Alexander Jenkins and, don't worry, I'm not going to bore you with another one of those pathetic poor-little-rich-boy yarns.

This is a small town and you all know who I am or I should say you all know who my father is. Is there anyone at this table who doesn't know the one and only Doctor James Rodney Jenkins? He's hot potatoes; fodder for the local rag. Small town, small hospital, small minds and small talk!

It's a Jenkins family tradition to make sure people in this town have something to talk about. I'll do my best in the telling not to diminish this fine custom.

It can't be too easy being on the board of Happy Haven Retirement Residence. I'm sure each one of you has a busy schedule but the thing is; it's a long story and I'm not sure where to begin.

I first met Charlie Gordon when I was a kid. He was a lawyer and he used to get drunk with my father, the good doctor, on Saturday nights. It was common knowledge in this town that Charlie got drunk on the other six nights of the week with a good variety of this fine town's upstanding citizens but on Saturday nights anybody looking for Charlie would find him playing poker at our house.

That first meeting and the many subsequent ones may not be worth wasting words on today. The encounter that matters is the most recent one that took place just three weeks ago.

I was here at Happy Haven as usual. I had to do split shifts that Tuesday. Hate working split shifts but don't let that news spoil your day. I can check my notes if you need an exact check-in time but as I remember it was about ten a.m. I was hoping to squeeze ten minutes out of the day for a coffee break when my father arrived with Charlie.

Charlie Gordon had no family. That's why Dr. Jenkins brought him in.

"He's all yours now, son," he said before handing me some papers; papers that I did not read.

I just gave them to the girl in admin when I passed her office door on my way to what was going to now be Charlie's room. My father didn't stick around; didn't want to waste his time talking to me, a son who was supposed to follow in his footsteps and be a big fish in a small pond just like him.

The fact that I'm a Personal Support Worker in a retirement home is an embarrassment to him. My daddy is one of the richest men in town and drives around in a fancy car with the big, black M-D on the license plate. He doesn't take kindly to people knowing that his only son makes ten bucks an hour looking after old folks who have somehow managed to out-live themselves.

So this day I forget about taking a coffee break. Instead I take Charlie's arm, walk him down the corridor to his room where I give him a hand to get settled in. I feel sorry for the poor bugger. I had no love for the guy. Everybody in town knew Charlie had been involved in his fair share of shady deals. And, just like everyone else, I knew he spent most of his nights with royalty, Crown Royal that is. Nothing but the best for Charlie. He made big bucks but he pissed most of it away as fast as he made it. Charlie is a drunk; an alcoholic and he should have been put into the hospital's rehab instead of into a retirement home.

But the good doctor didn't want Charlie in a rehab. No, sir! If Charlie ever sobered up he might just have a thing or two to say about Dr. Jenkins' involvement in some of those shady deals. Now I'm telling you this stuff but I'm also telling you there's no sense in letting any of this get into the hands of the local rag. That newspaper has had more than its fair share of crucifixions already and the town doesn't need another one. Charlie is dead. I think we can all agree to one thing because even an old, crooked drunk needs to rest in peace. I'm trusting you will keep your word and anything said in this board room stays in this room. Whatever he's done in his life is between him and his Maker now.

I didn't kill old Charlie. And if you handle this properly the way I know you can if you put your mind to it then we can all avoid any kind of trouble. Happy Haven Retirement Residence doesn't need bad publicity. The good doctor doesn't want to have to buy himself out of another scrape and I sure don't want to go to prison for a murder I did not commit.

So like I was saying I helped Charlie get settled into his room that morning. I was surprised over the next week or so to learn that he wasn't causing the trouble I thought he would. He seemed to get along with the other residents okay and I never heard any complaints about him from PSW's on other shifts. I didn't really have any trouble with Charlie either even though I knew something that nobody else in the residence knew.

Here's the secret. On my shift my father, the good doctor, was coming to visit Charlie every week or so. He would spend an hour or two visiting in Charlie's room and the two old codgers passed the time playing cards. Now he never visited Charlie on anybody else's shift; just mine. Why's that, you might be wondering. Well, I'll tell you why. Because when my father visited old Charlie the doctor always came into the residence carrying his old doctor's bag.

Now everybody knows doctors don't carry these big leather bags around anymore but old Dr. Jenkins wasn't someone who would be questioned about that any more than he is ever questioned about anything else. Now in that bag, if you were to look, you wouldn't find any stethoscope, lubricating jellies or diagnostic sets. No, sir! What you would find in that doctor's bag was a good supply of Crown Royal; good Canadian whiskey to keep old Charlie quiet.

Now that afternoon when Charlie wanted to go for a little walk, I couldn't see any good reason to say no. Charlie often went out for walks in the afternoon. He'd rarely stay out for more than a half hour and then he'd be back in his room and looking for his supper.

Sure he was drunk. But not so anybody would notice because Charlie was always drunk. The good doctor's ready supply of Crown Royal guaranteed that Charlie would not discover sobriety in his golden years.

Of course it was a cold day! It's winter for heaven's sakes. All the days are cold and we don't expect anything else in this northern climate. Charlie went out for afternoon walks on colder days than that one many times in the three weeks he lived here. Look, there may be a lot of things I am not good at. Sure, maybe I am not the best son and for sure I wouldn't make the best doctor. But I am a support worker and I'm damn good at what I do. You can ask anybody; ask the residents. Even Charlie would tell you I've been a good support to him if he could be here to tell you anything, God rest his soul.

That afternoon Charlie went out for his walk. Half an hour passed. He wasn't back. I didn't worry right away but when forty-five minutes went by and he still wasn't back in his room I made my report to admin. Weather had turned bad. Blizzard conditions were forecast. Police were notified and a search was started.

They didn't find him until late that night. Seems Charlie had walked over to the lakeside, set himself down at a picnic table and lost track of time. Now alcohol numbs the senses and thins the blood. Anyone under the influence would not recognize the warning signs of hypothermia. Seems Charlie drank some, got sleepy and lay down on the ground under the table where there wasn't so much snow. It took a few hours before cops in cruisers found his body covered in snow.

My father provided the Crown Royal. Is he the murderer?

Sure, I knew he went out for his walk that day same as any other day. Am I to blame? No, sir. You can't pin no murder on me.

Crown Royal killed Charlie. Make your arrest and make the charges stick if you can. Good luck to you!

WEAVING ALICE

Amos saw her for the first time at the local trade show. He had his book display table set up and had high hopes for his customary sales success. Her booth was directly across the wide aisle. He watched as she piled her table high with colourful woven placemats, scarves and afghans. The banner on the wall behind her table shouted, *"Weaving Alice"* in bold, black italic lettering. He had never seen a more striking, classic beauty. Neither could he force his eyes away from her dark olive complexion which was a complete contrast to his fat, freckled face. He pressed his tongue against the palatal implant, as he always did when feeling anxious. Amos did not know that his nervous habitual pushing changed his appearance to one closely resembling Marlon Brando in The Godfather.

When the arena doors opened to the public a sea of people blocked his view of Weaving Alice but this conundrum was miniscule in comparison to his desire. Amos made a silent vow to meet this unsuspecting woman by whatever means possible; the sooner the better.

If there was anything that Amos liked better than the sight of a beautiful female it was food. The joy he experienced when creating new recipes was what led him to becoming a moderately successful author of cookbooks which he sold at special events across the country just as he was doing this day in the arena of the small northern Ontario town.

Amos not only liked to cook, he loved to eat. Passionate about food, his voracious appetite and habitual manner of devouring multiple meals in a day could only be described as gluttony. A natural consequence of his over-indulgence was a bloated belly and a rotund rear-end. Amos was not a handsome man.

The fact that women were not attracted to him was of little consequence to Amos. If he wanted a woman in his life he would have her and Amos wanted Weaving Alice. He sat overlapping the cold, metal chair and with fat elbows resting on the table, Amos drew his hands together. He entwined his pudgy fingers to form a level ledge upon which he could rest his chins. From this comfortable vantage point he delighted in the glimpses he caught of her beauty across the crowded room.

As a young lad Amos had big blue eyes that often invited pats on the head and compliments such as, "What a handsome little man you are." Compliments were few and far between for him now that he had reached his middle years. Now these same eyes appeared washed out and skinny. The best they could do was to squint out over fat cheeks giving him the look of a nefarious criminal.

Amos knew that his general appearance was not one that attracted lovely women the caliber of Weaving Alice. He emitted an audible girlish giggle as he allowed himself to remember the arrogant Annabelle and the pouty Patricia. They had not wanted to be with him either. Nor had the teasing Theresa or the myriad other women who thought they were too good for him. Bitches! He had shown them! Amos was not a man to be ignored.

As much as he wanted to sell copies of his cookbooks, his annoyance grew greater throughout the morning with customers who stopped to tell him all about their cooking successes and failures. The incessant seeking of advice and expectation of personalized autograph in a cookbook bugged him. Amos wanted to yell, "Take your book and scram.

You're blocking my view!" But he practiced restraint and gifted his adoring public with what he believed was a charming smile; not the grimacing grin a mirror would have reflected.

Just before noon there was a lull in activity. His stomach growled. He reached down and pulled the cooler out from under his display table. He ignored the neatly wrapped roast beef sandwiches he had made the night before. Those he would eat later. What was more important to him than his hunger was his determination to impress the beautiful Alice. He lifted the oval serving plate from the cooler and laid it on the table behind a high pile of cookbooks. Beneath the saran wrap covering the plate was an attractive array of smoked salmon, imported European crackers, gourmet cheeses from France, Italy, and Switzerland. There were grapes both green and purple. *No woman can refuse such delights,* Amos thought.

He used great care in removing the saran. He didn't want to disturb the colourful pattern he had created with precision earlier that morning. He watched. He waited. At last the aisle between him and his victim was clear. The time was right. Serving plate held high, waiter fashion, and with the unexpected smoothness of a much slimmer man, Amos carried his bulk across the cold, concrete arena floor. In his left hand he held a small luncheon plate and a soft blue cotton dinner napkin.

He was standing in front of her display table in silence. He watched as she wove her needle, which carried the silver thread, in and out. On her lap rested a delicate silk tapestry in the making.

"Beautiful!" he said.

She raised her head from her work and offered a cool but polite smile in response to his compliment.

"I've been admiring your work from across the aisle," Amos continued. "I'm Chef Amos Bortelli. I've come prepared with some delicacies that I trust you will allow me to share with you." With a slight bow he proffered the serving tray. "Please join me in a little light lunch."

With swift skill he extended his left hand leaving her no option but to accept the luncheon plate and napkin.

"Well, maybe just a little," she responded.

Amos held the serving plate as she selected until her plate was a tempting garden of colour.

"Thank you. My name is Alice Weaver."

"The name is Weaver and not Weaving?" he asked.

"Weaving is my passion. My surname is just coincidence."

"My dear Alice, there is no coincidence. There is reason for everything." He smiled his wicked smile.

His comment alerted Alice Weaver causing her to take a closer look at this stranger bearing gifts. Her eyes drew his totality into her memory, into her heart and into her talented hands. She decided that she would enjoy the food for now. Later she would do what needed to be done.

They shared the food until the oval serving plate was empty. Then her gaze left his face and returned along with her nimble fingers to the tapestry.

"Alice. May I join you for a few moments before our day here ends?"

Alice did not look up from her work. She merely nodded her head in assent.

"Thank you," he said. He gathered up the plates and returned to his book table where by now a few people were waiting to have their cookbooks autographed.

Amos was a Cheshire cat as he conducted his book signing that afternoon. He thought of how he would carry out his ingenious plan. When the Trade Show finished that day he would invite Alice home for dinner. She would accept his invitation. No woman had ever refused a dinner invitation from Chef Bortelli. He visualized his kitchen. He saw himself reaching out for the sharp carving knife. His excitement was building. Yes, his cooking fame would be enough to entice her. He would succeed in his plot to rid the earth of yet another arrogant bitch who thought she was too good to date a fat man. He felt wonderful.

Alice Weaver's afternoon quickly passed. She made many sales. The scarves and the placemats were popular. She sold only one afghan and wondered if she had priced them too high. Whenever she was not busy with a customer Alice would send her deliberate gaze across the aisle where she rested it upon the face of Amos Bortelli. After a few seconds she would return her attention to the skillful silk weaving of the tapestry.

At five o'clock the trade show was over. Vendors throughout the arena were packing up their unsold wares. Amos had few books to take home. He could carry everything in one shopping bag that conveniently fit inside his cooler leaving him with only the large cooler on wheels to drag out to his vehicle.

He watched Alice as she carefully folded and packed up her woven goods into a large cardboard carton. Now was the time to make his move. Pulling the cooler behind him he once again crossed the aisle.

"Hello again, Alice. I trust your day was prosperous."

"Yes, thank you," she responded automatically not stopping her work for even a second to smile or continue the conversation.

Amos was used to being ignored. "May I help you with your packing?" he offered.

"No thanks. I'm nearly finished."

"That's going to be quite a heavy box. Let me give it a ride atop my cooler out to the parking lot."

She hesitated but only for a second. "Thank you, yes."

"Do you want to put the tapestry you are working on into the box too, Alice?"

"No, this will fit nicely into my large handbag. I keep it with me always when I'm outside my home.

I'm often inspired to weave into my tapestry those things that need to be dealt with."

"Dealt with?" he asked.

"It's just a catch-all phrase I tend to use too often."

They walked through the arena to the exit. In the parking lot the first car they came to was the one belonging to Amos.

"This is mine. Where are you parked, Alice?"

"Just a few cars down."

"I will wheel your box to your car then, shall I?"

"If you don't mind. Thanks again."

"No problem."

They came to Alice's Honda Civic where Amos placed the large cardboard box into the trunk. He said good-bye and began to walk back to his own vehicle pulling his red cooler behind him.

"Could I have been wrong? Oh, surely not, she thought. I'm never wrong about these things."

She stepped away from the back of her car and was just about to open its door when she heard him shout, "Oh, Alice, just a moment!"

"Hmm, I thought so!"

She watched as Amos retraced his steps. Once he was standing directly before her he asked, "I know it is presumptuous of me since we barely know each other but surely you have heard of me and my infamous cookbook. Would you do me the honour of coming to my home for dinner?"

For just a second Alice seemed to hesitate. She threw her head back and stared up into the summer sky.

While she did so, the hint of a smile appeared on her face.

Amos was not blind to the up tilt of her lips. *The arrogant bitch thinks she's got me in the palm of her hand. Good! That's exactly what I want her to think.*

"You're a devil, Amos!" She smiled. "I will accept your invitation."

He had never doubted that she would. They always did.

"Just leave your car here, Alice. I'll drive you to my home. After dinner I'll bring you back here to pick up your car if that's okay with you."

"No, I'll follow you, Amos. That way I'll just drive myself home after dinner."

"As you wish," he responded as he began to think about how he would ditch her car once the deed was done.

It was a short drive. Amos pulled into the driveway of a large white house situated well back from the street.   A covered verandah ran the width of the front of the house. The neighbours on either side were a good distance away. The home of Amos Bortelli was barely seen by the neighbours across the street sheltered as it was by two large Maples on the front, hedged lawn.

Alice pulled her car in behind his. While he drove his car straight into the garage she parked in the driveway. He closed the garage door then, keys in hand; he walked toward his front door. He turned the key, swung the door open and Alice stepped into a large foyer.

"Welcome to my home. Come this way, Alice," he said as he walked through a doorway into a spacious living-room.

Clutching her large handbag Alice followed him and sat on a chair.

"Red or white for you, Alice?" he asked.

"Oh, I don't drink wine as a rule."

"Very well. Would you care for some juice or perhaps just a glass of water?"

"All right, then," she decided. "Wine it will be and let's make it red."

"Wonderful! Make yourself comfortable, Alice. I'll be back with the wine in a jiffy."

Alice reached into her handbag and withdrew the tapestry she was in the process of creating. She began smoothly slipping the silver thread through the silk.

In the kitchen Amos busied himself. He drew the carving knife out of its stand. Its gleaming sharp blade thrilled him as he ran his fat fingers up and down along its sides. He thought about where he would bury the pieces once the deed was done. He plotted how he would get her car out of his neighbourhood. Confident of success he dropped the small tablet into the red wine.

She was busy with needle and thread when he returned to the living-room.

"Drink this, my dear." He handed her the wine-filled crystal stemware.

"Thank you, Amos. Please place it on the table while I get this tapestry back into my purse."

"Enjoy your drink, Alice. And while you are doing so I will begin to prepare a feast fit for a queen."

With anticipation Amos returned to the kitchen. He put a few hors d'oeuvres onto a silver tray. He lifted the sharp carving knife from the counter once again. He would do as he had always done in the past with all the other arrogant bitches who thought they were too good for him. He would wait until the drink had put her to sleep. Then he would carry her into the basement where he could take his time disrobing her. He would do with her whatever he desired and when he was tired of his games he would begin carving her up. It was in the carving that his senses screamed in delight. He could hardly wait.

He returned to the living-room, tray in hand. He could see that Alice was still intent on her needlework. She had not had much wine to drink, if any at all.

"May I tempt you with these?" he asked with a devilish grin.

"Thank you, Amos. Just place them on the coffee table and I will enjoy them with my wine."

Pleased with her response Amos placed the silver tray on the coffee table and then plunked his large girth onto the sofa across from the chair in which Alice continued to sew. She will drink the wine, he thought. I'll be patient. It's just a matter of time.

He sat on the sofa and looked across the room at her lovely face. Her beauty is almost angelic, he thought.

Alice looked up from her needlework and returned his gaze. Then she lowered her eyes and stared at his large feet, his fat trousered legs. Her hands were working with lightning speed now as she stared at his solar plexus, his chest and his throat.

Amos felt very strange. This woman's gaze was making him feel something he had never experienced before. He felt powerless. His skinny eyes looked down. How was it possible? His chest, his belly; his entire body had disappeared. He moved his arms to feel his own girth. He felt the movement but at the same time there were no arms to see. He was under her spell.

The hands of Alice Weaver were now holding a tapestry that was so large it covered her knees and spread out onto the carpeted floor.

Through skinny eyes Amos peered at the tapestry.

For just a moment Alice stopped the flow of the silver thread through the silk fabric. She stopped just long enough for Amos to see the pattern of his bulky body.

With horror he raised his eyes and stared at Alice. She began to sew again.

His mouth opened and he cried, "Spare me!"

He once more looked down upon the tapestry. He could see one of his eyes now. His voice was gone. And then he could see no more."

Alice looked down upon her completed tapestry.

"Are you there, God?" she asked.

"I'm here, Alice Weaving. Well done, my child!"

"Oh, but there is always another one, God! Always another evil force to be dealt with."

"Yes, that's true, my child," God replied. "Perhaps giving humans free will was not my most wise decision."

"Will I be returning to you now, Lord, or do you have another assignment to send me on?" Alice asked.

"You deserve a break, Alice. Come with me now."

"Yes, Lord." Alice sighed as she gathered up the silk tapestry, folded it neatly and placed it into her large handbag. She surveyed the living-room and said good-bye to the place where evil deeds had claimed the lives of many unsuspecting women.

"What of the car in the driveway, Lord?"

"Oh, yes. It wouldn't take you long, would it, Alice?"

"No, Lord. You go. I won't be far behind you."

Alice walked out of the house. She took a long hard look at the parked vehicle, removed two needles and some thread from her handbag. It took her no time at all and the driveway was bare.   Alice looked at the

second, smaller tapestry. "I had a car just like this one

when I was a human on earth," she recalled, before she

folded the fabric neatly and tucked it away in her

handbag.

Author's Bio:

Audrey Austin was born and raised by her parents in Toronto, Ontario, Canada. At an early age she married and before long her two daughters arrived. Having only a high school education she waited until her children were grown before going back to school. She attended University of Toronto and later graduated from Transformational Arts College. She has lived in Toronto & its suburbs; Prince Edward Island and in New Zealand. She has enjoyed other international travel but only as a tourist in countries such as Thailand; Korea; Bahamas; Bermuda; Columbia, Puno and Cartagena in South America. She always wanted to write and did so in a small way as a hobby but never made any attempt at publication. It was not until she retired at an uncertain age that she finally made the promise to herself that she would fulfill her dream of being an author. She loves creative writing and how can something one loves so much be classified as work? She has written novels, novellas, and short stories always doing her best to keep up with the characters. Audrey is currently living in Elliot Lake, Ontario, Canada.

http://www.amazon.com/author/audreyaustin

http://www.facebook.com/audreyaustinca